AF291042

BENGT GH NILSSON

Alone in Kleptomania

Tryck och förlag: BoD

ISBN: 978-91-7463-768-7

<u>Escape</u>

Through its increasingly weeping eyes she saw train slowly disappear behind. The building, the platforms and the entire track area dissolved in the shimmering fields of grayish-brown tones and distorted perspectives. Hopelessly alone, she stood at the back of the last car. Newly trail aboard the long train from Nanjing tentative rattled through the last track switches. Now back on the road after a short stop in Hengyang. In order to harvest the last bit of the long journey down to Guangzhou.

With hands constantly drying away their mocking tears, it was clear to her that now there was no turning back. She was irreversibly on its way out. Her despair and tears filled chest pain was reinforced by traces of cormorants increasingly rapid thumping. As well as the increasing awareness of what she left behind. While uncertainty about the future increasingly imposing themselves on.

Just a few hours earlier had now almost seventeen-year-old Yin Woo made the crucial decision and during the night secretly filled the family's worn-out old suitcase with a few hurriedly selected clothes. Packed some food and the bare essentials and then as quietly as possible to leave the house. With agonizing step taken his bicycle in the shed. Fastened the bag on the carrier and with a few quick turn of the pedals before the astonished even sleepy oxen and anxiously cackling ducks disappeared off into the darkness. After quickly rolled down the hill on the bumpy gravel road she stepped on in the damp cool morning air. A meandering bike ride through fields of tobacco plantations along the eight-kilometer long and winding road to the bus station. The moon hung like a gayamelon beyond the mountains, and all the stars enveloped her like a twinkling ceiling. If it had not been for the tragic circumstances, everything would have seemed like a fairytale night. After a few minutes passed the turnoff to the farm, where her unsuspecting love lived. Namely two years older Jianyu, which she only talked to on a few occasions. Such as when she and her mother sometimes been there and bought fresh vegetables.

It was already here, when thoughts of her secret love suddenly appeared, as doubts stopped her slightly. Looked long away towards the farm while the pedals could rest a while. The up hills then felt extra long and heavy, but not even the thoughts of Jianyu could stop her. She had decided. It was today it would happen. Otherwise, probably never. Now it was not to be sentimental.

Easy sweaty after the long bike ride to the village Gouzishan she puffed out at the bus stop. The sky had almost brightened. At least, so much so that one could glimpse the mountains away on the horizon. Took a few refreshing and much needed sips from water bottle. Before she carefully chained his bicycle on the outskirts of the already chock full cycle instead. Did the bus to the Hengyang Railway Station went relatively often. Sat therefore on the ground next to await it. Nice back leaning against a pile of sleepers who stood there for some reason. Still strong tar-scented. Together they formed nearly a board. Small and cute as she was with her beautiful eyes. Their regular dainty Chinese characteristics and his long black but a little flygiga hair. Now lightly swaying in the still cool morning breeze.

It was only in Hengyang, when the noisy and smelly diesel bus passed the breathtakingly high bridge over Yangtsifloden that realization came. Namely, how terribly lonely she was. Despite all the people and cars jostling with each other. For the first time in his soon as the 17-year life, she was completely self-contained town. A spectrum of her unusual smells from city jostling with each other in the nose. There were fumes and smells from restaurants and snack bars. Sweaty people and perfumes in a mix. Aromas that are not normally available in rural areas to the same extent. For her, an exotic blend of aromas. A palpable sense that you were in a big city and no longer remain among tobacco plantations in the country. An emerging concern in the stomach, however, began more and more to make itself felt. Like when their footing in a habitual and secure existence is being lost. Yet confidently unaware that that feeling would in time prove to be mildly justified.

The bus finally stopped at the train station. More than satisfied with the final bumping piece of downtown's crooked and worn paving stones. Alone and with uncertain steps she lugged away with the suitcase toward the main entrance. Reacted with surprise at all busy people running here and there. Felt increasingly Mills Place and bortkommen. A feeling that was reinforced by the strong speaker sound that echoed between the walls inside the station hall. Also took the opportunity to purchase some extra victuals in one of the kiosks there. Two cans of Coke and a triangular skinksandwich wrapped in plastic. While a cheese sandwich happened ended in her pocket. Almost like just by itself ...!? Without paying for the course. Oddly enough, without giving her a guilty conscience either. Just thought she wanted a sandwich to. However, it was not that obvious offense against the home's moral education, which then made her think of her mother. No, it struck her just that soon ... or maybe already ... they should have discovered the empty bed. ... Yin Yin, the mother would surely have cried. Even irritated as usual. A little harsh as she was in the morning. Van that usually do not get an immediate response from her on the verge of unconsciousness sleepy daughter. So ... even naively unaware that this morning would change life at home. Just a short time left before the realization of Yin's disappearance would overturn everything. A future scenario that nobody in the family had anticipated.

Unstructured and aimless as Yin often was invited because the last night, nor on a few more occasions, to complement the clothing luggage. That is to say, no more than T-shirts and underwear previously packed into a bag.Along with a bottle of water and other necessities. Coat shortage was a Minde problems so far. Where the railway station is now on its way from the ticket office. LUG on his bad conscience, suitcase and their dearly bought the train ticket. She, the young little girl from the country, at all could afford such a train ticket. Yes, it depended solely on the mother-saving box in the cupboard already the night before länsats on its entire capital. Namely, all the 840 yuan in notes that were there. The entire bundle, she had carelessly stuffed into the pocket. While they have been replaced with a red flower in the casket. A sort of compensation and desperate gesture with the hope of forgiveness. A tender-hearted attempt to show compassion. In order to so brazenly and hårdhudat seized his own mother only savings. Money over a long period of self-denial and with great effort scraped together.Now decimated to zero. After his prank she crept unnoticed back to her and her still sleeping brother's room. With the realization that the plan as far gone as anticipated.

When the approaching train eventually slid into the station in Hengyang, she felt a mixture of anxiety and excitement. Her pink-way ticket to the train number G1101 she constantly looked at had cost her the whole 180 yuan.A considerable part of travel funds. The signs on the platform, she realized that her place should be in the last wagon. Slightly stressed by the train screeching brakes and the speaker monotone female voice echoing she thrust herself forward, however, between the second waiting passengers. Half running and dragging it to her large suitcase she took over the platform back along the train. Decided to board the wagon front entrance. Her legs shook slightly. Not by the effort of the three steps up. But most of the awareness that it was the first time in her life, she stepped aboard a train. Somewhat confused and uncertain, yet proud of herself she went back through the carriage. There was already relatively many travelers. But still some empty seats left. Was looking for a seat 5A. Which fortunately turned out to be a window seat. Quite happy with the location marked her chair as busy with the bag.

Many of the other passengers looked rather tired and bored. Where they were scattered here and there in the carriage. However, immediately noticed the musty and stuffy air in the passenger compartment and waited, therefore, to understand. Instead went out to the little separate space in the far back. Where the door to the platform was still open. Still with a restless supervisory glance at the bag in the passenger compartment. A light and cool morning breeze penetrated through the doorway. More noticeable after the last of the boarding passengers boarded. She breathed in ... and breathing out. Tried to collect himself after all the impressions that have already passed the revue during the remarkable morning. Anyone who has just become the first chapter of her new free life.

When the doors closed and the squeaking long train again moved forward, she stood still for a long while at the trailer rear window and thought. After a moment of contemplation and examination of the breakup of the home, she went back to her place. Wiped away some tears from her cheek. Moved the bag to the chair next and sat by the window. Quickly looked at the clock showed 9:10. Then let his gaze wander along downtown's skyline. All high-rise buildings in the horizon that slowly floated past. Felt dazed while empty inside. Somehow still comfortable with their decision. Consider, finally taking the courage to me and left it there misery, she thought. For the first time has taken its own position, and then make it a reality. Self realize it, she does not even have dreamed of just a year ago. Admittedly, with sadness but of their own free will. A decision that ultimately did not find any other solution. With almost incomprehensible strength left his home and his own family. The mother, her brother Zhinsun and of course ... stepfather. Namely, that which was the cause of everything. The hatred grew within her, only she thought of him. If she had not given up by now, maybe even the man's own life was in danger. Not at all incredible in view of Yin's hot temper and unconditional desire for revenge.

The sleeping lady in the park opposite had now opened his eyes and smiled at her. Still with the book in her lap after the nap. Although her hair graying slightly, she looked very youthful and respectable. Nice makeup and almost a little coquettish with its colorful silky blouse. With matching shiny black midjeskärp to the short black skirt. A sparkling necklace around his neck and on his feet a pair of shiny and probably expensive black leather shoes. She examined the Yin top down. However, without showing what she was thinking. Listed sure the rural fabric and the worn sports shoes. But it seemed apparently still untouched. Leaned forward and said in a low voice curious
-   Where this lonely young girl to go today?

- I'm going to Guangzhou, said Yin with determined
voice. Almost as if to underline that this was not an unusual situation for her.
- I understand ... and ... what will you do there
then. Work may !?

Yin knew instinctively that this was precisely nothing
that this lady had something to do. But, not wanting to
be rude, and therefore came to a spontaneous and un-
planned lie.

- I'll ... be ... to visit my grandmother, she said, and
took a swig from the water bottle.
- Oh, how nice. Then secure your grandmother will be
happy, right.
- Mmm, she replied a bit hesitantly. Easy concerned that
the lady would continue its hearing.
- Yes, I will also to Guangzhou. Lives namely there. Has
been in the top Nanjing ... little shops ... you could
say. It will be nice to sleep in his own bed again, she said,
and laughed some more done.
- Where in the city live your grandmother?
- She ... I do not remember exactly, but I have the address in the bag.
- Has she might like me lived a long time in Guangzhou?
- Excuse me ... I just have to, she said, and stood
up. Hesitated a bit but then went back in the carriage.

- Hey ... Miss! The toilet is the other way, 'said the lady pleasantly instructive.

Yin did not answer but simply turned on his heel. Went irritable the other direction. Staggering through the aisle of the train's growing body roll. Found once the toilet at the other end of the carriage, where the door was unfortunately locked. During his anticipation she took the opportunity to distance closer study of the fancy but somewhat uncomfortable curious lady. Was not used to being spoken to by strangers just like that. Felt some discomfort indeed. Suddenly she sees, however, the lady leans forward. How she tries to read the suitcase docket !? Yin froze and tried to remember what was there. Though really, she had no idea. Probably mother's name and address, she thought ...!? But why is she so interested? Or perhaps just generally curious? Yin did not know, but it gave her still a disturbing feeling. Did not think anyone would be interested in the bag. Was interrupted, however, in his thoughts when a woman with a small child just came out of the toilet. Finally it was her turn.

- I kept an eye on your bag, meanwhile, said the lady, when Yin once sat in its place.
- You never know. There are so many who steals things nowadays.

Yin smiled indifferently back towards the lady. While she noted with relief that the docket was actually quite smooth. Neither the name or address. She breathed out. Then sat with closed eyes and the comfort of the chair.Ceded Spirit as if she were tired and just got the urge to sleep. Anything not to be confronted with some more questions. You never know what she is looking for, thought Yin confused and leaned to the side. However squinted slightly through their eyes closed. Did that lady shot down his glasses from the hairline. Took the book from her lap and continued to read. Seems to have understood the hint after all, thought Yin. Also felt the fatigue came over her. It had been a stressful morning in many ways. And now wanted the brain not to go. It was two and a half hours left to Guangzhou and train monotonous vocals over the track did, she soon fell asleep.With hand secured against your suitcase and head diagonally toward the headrest, she left their home behind. Both in reality and in mind. Did the mother in front of him. The small woman of habit always combed in camellia oil in your hair in the morning and then put it up in a knot. An old tradition of Xiang Tang neighborhood from where she originally came. Belonged really Miaofolket and prac-ticed still a part of their customs and traditions.Among other things, they dressed in very colorful clothes on festive occasions. A heritage Yin himself was not going to manage and pass on. She imagined anyway ...!?

Awakened by the train suddenly stopped with a jerk. Did not understand where she was. I realized then that the train stopped at a station. What, you could not see. Looked at the clock. Five of the ten. Thus had slept for a while. Heard people in the distance talking to each other. Someone door slammed. Otherwise there was silence in the carriage. It seemed as if some fellow passengers also dozed off.

After a while suddenly opened the front door. Two uniformed men came into the cart. Yin felt his heart hammering in his chest. When she realized that it was not actually the conductor. Breathing was also uneven and the thoughts rushed through her head. For suddenly it dawned on her ... two policemen. It is not possible, she thought. To those at home understood everything and have already figured out that she was here. On board the train.And on this particular train additionally. No, it could not be. Time stood still. Slowly they walked back through the carriage and eyed each passenger. Yin tried to look as unconcerned as possible and for some reason she concealed suitcase with his shirt ...!? Even when she cards encountered one of the policemen's sharp gaze, she stressed unconsciously concern over the bag ... for some reason ...!? They continued further back in my time and nothing more happened. Not until the door at the back struck again, she dared turn around and look. She breathed out. But at the same time wondered what they actually did there? On this particular train. Had absolutely no idea, and the lady opposite was not available for any questions Had namely fallen asleep again. Sitting just as before with the book in his lap and his glasses perched on his forehead.

Eventually heard Yin a whistle sounded and shortly thereafter began to train slowly moving. Significantly relieved after the incident, she took off her warm footwear. Snuggled up with her legs in the seat and made himself more at ease. Also felt more alert now after the nap. Took out Coca-Cola and sandwiches. She was thirsty and really enjoyed the drink. Coke! Had only drunk it a few times before. Only when they have been included in Hengyang and acted or so. But from now she could actually drink, just what she wanted. Just such a thing.

The view through the window changed character as the train wound its way through the Chinese countryside down to Guangzhou. The sandwiches slim down quickly. But the thoughts in her head was no longer in the present but hovered helplessly back toward Gouzishan. Against the small farm where, among the tobacco plantations. Against the mother, her nine year old brother, all the animals, stepfather and ... well, the whole life that played out there with both joy and anguish. That which for nearly the entire seventeen years had been her home. But only until today. The day that now would be the turning point in her young life. The unknown life that just only begun.

It was with grief, she thought back to the last two years. At the time when the stepfather and her relationship gradually deteriorated. Everything escalated when he submitted an application to the school. Without Yin's knowledge in addition. Namely an official request to Yin would have quit secondary school early. And instead work on the farm. Everything came to light when he at breakfast one morning threw up some sort of stamped certification on the table. And while just blurted out, you do not go to school anymore. From today you should stay home and work with us. The mother was a bit further away but said nothing. Had too much respect for him.Moreover probably thought she too, that it was needed more help at home. In their toil in tobacco production.

You will namely work in the drying house. Make sure that the fire constantly kept alive, he explained brusquely. It is not too hard, added the mother in an attempt to comforting. Admittedly, it is hot and you can expect long hours, but it could be worse, she continued. We have a lot of work now and is really too few to cope with it. Yin sat silent. Most, however, astonished by what she suddenly heard. Staring desperately down in the table.Looked at his cup of green tea and the half-eaten piece of bread. Did not even see on that certificate. Already understood all too clearly what mattered. No more school ...!? There, she finally began to enjoy as well. Just could not understand. Probably no point in protesting either, she thought. They have now decided all that ... with the principal and so ... what can I do about it? Nothing! Felt his eyes moistened. Tears which penetrated against her will. Did not turn out weak, but left the breakfast in anger and ran out. The only sound was the door that fought back with a deafening bang. The mother sighed loudly and from the stepfather came some kind of grunting murmur. It seemed as if both had anticipated the reaction. They knew, of course, that Yin would rather go to school. And precisely because it had everything done in secret. Without her involvement and transparency. Something they later might have to pay a very high price for.

Time passed and the days in the drying house was often long and tedious. Sometimes she also had night shift. But complaining is not outward but collected instead on a kind of anger inside. Tried forget school altogether.Devoted himself instead to daydreaming. An often practiced method to endure a forced life. Especially when boredom settles tight around one. When freedom itself as caught in a net. Dreamed instead about life there.Somewhere ... far away. A life she knew was there. Although it now seemed out of reach. Played with different scenarios for its future. There in solitude in front of the warm fireplace. Did, however, that life would take a different turn a beautiful day. It was in any case there, she imagined and hoped for. A compelling expectation that was born out of her rebellious personality, young age and the obvious will to live.

The relationships in the family and particularly between Yin and stepfather grew increasingly worse. Often they quarreled and shouted at each other. Things were thrown and doors slammed. It even happened on a few occasions, she received slaps and punches. Despite the mother's gentle and helpless protests. But often Yin too tired to make a fuss. For some days she must be to go up already at five o'clock in the morning. In protest against the pouting her way through the days. Sometimes half-asleep out there in the dryer housing trapped heat. Except when she had time to play with Zhinsun course. Then you could everyday forgotten for a while. Could again become that fun and life affirming girl with a twinkle in his eye. Whoever she's always been, before his stepfather came into their lives. Especially before that late evening when he came home drunk and angry. Back after being drunk and with some other farmers in the area. Probably even gambled away their money. When he woke up the mother and threatened her with his gun. With precisely the weapon that Yin since often thought to throw in the lake. Her little brother however was the most carefree type. Perhaps the most because of their age but also their nature. Had indeed not yet been confronted with life's increasing anguish. Thankfully for him, she thought.

Yin came abruptly back to reality. A conductor did loudly their entrance into the cart. She immediately took off her pink ticket and waited their turn. This was almost too exciting for her. All that she had not experienced before felt so interesting and pleasurable in any way. Looked down at his watch. Already 10:20 and barely one hour left to Guangzhou, she thought expectantly. Keep in mind, once I'm there. Dream will become true. And ... she did not want to wake up from it. Got his hole in the ticket and stuffed happy down in his little wallet. This is going well. So far mostly gone smoothly, she thought, and smiled at the joke.

At only half an hour left of the train suddenly there came a phone. The coquettish lady opposite looked dazedly up and started looking in her purse. "Madame Biyu" ... she answered shortly. Listened attentively, and commenting now and then with the words ... "Yes ...

yes ... yes." Since she finished the conversation with ...
"quarter past eleven when" ... and put the phone back in
the bag. While she gave Yin a big smile and said ...

- My, how time has run away. We're almost there. It gets
a bit boring with long train journeys, right !?
- Yeah.
- In the past I used to always fly but have become so
afraid of flying. Goofy is there really. Really do not
know why it is like that with the years. But you're not
afraid? In order to fly, I mean.

Yin was not prepared for the question. She, who never
even seen an airplane up close. Much less been in
one. She did not know if she was afraid or not, but
said ...

- Well, a little scared I might ... well.
- Well, I do not know, but to ride the train's not completely safe, from what you've heard. By the way ... if
you want, you can ride with me in the car to your
grandmother. My driver will namely fetch me at the station. So you will not have to take the subway or
taxi. There is always a bit awkward and stressful, when
you come to the 'big city'. Would not it be a good fit for
you? If she does not live too far away ... to say?
- Joooo ... said Yin while the brain was working at full
speed. It there with her grandmother was just invent-

ed. But on the other hand ... if she could get a free-ride, so why not.
- OK! If ... there is not too big hassle ... then?
- No not at all. We travel so much unnecessary anyway here and there. How well! Then we say so, 'said the lady and gave her her infectious smile again. By the way what is your name? There have I not asked.
- Yin ... my name is ...
- And I'm Madame Biyu. You can call me Madame.
- Well ...

Suddenly, just things happened. Such as herself no longer seemed to have control over. So it felt. It just happened that it became simply. Strange !? Maybe life is like this, she thought. That things just happen and you ... flowing with as well. But then hey, personal driver ...!? Who can afford it? What is this lady really? Yin had no grandmother. Not alive, anyway. It all was a white lie. But her predetermined plan was still, to somehow get to a particular address in Guangzhou. Whoever she had written down on a small patch and brought from home. And hopefully, also remained in the wallet.

Guangzhou

Almost exactly ten past eleven in the morning rolled the train from Nanjing into the station. The east of the ones in Guangzhou. It was a beautiful October day and the electronic thermometer on the platform proved to +24 degrees. When the two come out of the train and down on the platform, waved the lady, or Madame Biyu which she apparently called himself, a man was heading towards them. It would soon prove to be her chauffeur. He also presented as the Yin. And she herself for the man who "country girl" Madame. Without any hesitation, he grabbed Madame's chic little cerisfärgade bag on wheels. With Yin brown and unsightly ugly suitcase in the other hand, he went before them through the station building. Away towards the outside waiting car. Yin looked wide-eyed around him. Could hardly believe she was really here. The great hall, all people, all the sounds and colorful advertising on large TVs. Felt overwhelmed and now to top it all off with a man who was carrying her bag. What was this ... ?? Just seven or eight hours ago she was home in bed, and now she was in the middle of this. In Guangzhou! Madame Biyu noticed how bortkommen she looked out and asked, laughing, how it felt. If everything was ok, and so on. Was however only one amazed nodding response back. Where obviously speechless in the current session. Mentally af-

flicted with a kind of "overflow" of all the new impressions.

Never had she seen such a polished car in his
life. Obviously knew not that it was a Mercedes 500, but
experienced only sight a large black and fantastically
nice car. The driver opened the doors for the ladies, and
then placed the bags in the trunk. When the doors
closed again if they got Yin almost a feeling of having
gone to heaven. Everything was silenced. Found himself
suddenly in a soft and elegant black leather sofa smell-
ing of exclusivity. The interior was in sober dull colors
with shiny wood strips everywhere. A dashboard as if it
were taken from a space shuttle. Such as Zhinsun had
several photos of the wall at home.

Madame Biyu sat in the front seat. Brought down the
sun visor with vanity mirror, while a lamp lit. Opened
her handbag and sminketuiet. Screwed then up the lipstick to touch up the hue slightly. It could, after all, have
been too little of the bloody hue. Even sprayed some
perfume behind the ears. Yin had the whole backseat to
himself, felt almost like a princess. What was that for
the address that your little grandmother lived on, wondered Madame, when the driver started the car. Yin
took up his note from the wallet. But just when she
would hand it over, had a problem. The very name she
did not show. It was a man's name, and no grandmother

can be called that. Therefore, she tore of the uppermost part of the name of. Madame Biyu took the note and read the address. Number 119 Kengkou Road. It is not so far from here, right? The driver shrugged but typed in the address of the buttons in the built-in GPS 'one. A map in color quickly came up on the screen. Then a voice that said ... "Go straight on and next to the right". Yin followed the astonishing progress on the screen with great interest and surprise. Had never seen anything like it. Felt like pure magic while the car almost silently slipped away through the city. The only sound was a so-called traditional Chinese instrumental chanson as very weak poured out of the speakers. The sidewalks were filled with people, many of whom were surprisingly young. Where are all the older people, she considered, while Madame was talking to the driver. Yin could not even listen. Was too fascinated by everything she saw through the car's windows.

The streets became gradually narrower and addresses any more worn. Also noticed that people are more and more looked curiously at the car. It's probably not a dozen to be in this part of town, she thought. Felt almost a bit peculiar and proud there in the back seat. Imagine if you came home in such a here and turned up at the farm. While they could only believe that there were some senior politicians from Beijing that had gone wrong. She was stopped, however, in their minds, for shortly thereafter swung the driver toward the sidewalk. Announced Madame Biyu that now they arrive at the current address. Yin looked around and noted small shops, businesses and cafes. Certainly not an environment on par with Madame Biyus class, yet she turned with a smile and said ...

- Well Yin, now you finally arrive at your grand mother. Nice huh '?! It went well this. You might recognize you?
- Well, now it was a while since I was here but ...
- Yes, but it is number 119 up there at the house, so it is true enough.
- M mmm ...! ??
☐
Both the driver and Madame stepped out of the car. The boot lid opened itself and there lay her brown and worn suitcase in all its simplicity. Somewhat out of place in this particular car, perhaps, but still. The driver lifted it with ease and the door closed itself also itself naturally. As stylish as it had just opened. Yin bowed and thanked hands together in front of him. Madame did the same and gave Yin a long affectionate hug. Wished her luck and asked her grandmother's health. Also got her pale purple business cards. Emphasized that if she ever possibly needed a job or otherwise wanted help, so it was just to touch. She would remember ... "girl from the country." Yin

thanked for the business card and everything she had done for her. Even without even asking or begging for it. Is not it odd, she thought. But perhaps there are such people everywhere. In addition to the home country of course. Where are all so stubborn and head-strong. Sputters most at each other.

Madame Biyu sat down in the front seat. Closed the door and waved happily to the Yin while the car slowly whisked away away and disappeared at the next cross street. There she stood now ...!? Long and petrified in a cloud of Madame's wonderful perfume. As a bortkommen girl in the big city. Still with business card in hand and suitcase beside him. For a long time viewing them. Barely noticed the motorcycle as deafening roared past her at one meter distance. Not until after a long while was the awareness of the environment more tangible. If the people who passed by. If the curious men that scouting was sitting in a puff of smoke on the patio right next door. If the relatively high, and almost worn shabby houses on both sides of the street. Heard even a bird chirp somewhere. Probably from the top of the trees that adorned the sidewalk. Knew their despair even the smell of cooked food. Hungry as she already become like this in the middle of the day. But now there was no mother here. No forward succumbed delicacies on the table. But now she was standing all alone on a street in Guangzhou and knew neither in or out. Looked a bit desperate down on the business card. Which read: Madame Biyu Choi Hardy, Chairman of the Board, Canton divertissement. With the address in both Guangzhou and Paris ...!? Not that she understood that much, but one thing was clear. This is no ordinary woman. Not even here in Guangzhou, she thought in amazement. Also realized the business card was worth saving. One never knew ?!

Yin could never go completely straight with that big suitcase. Was as always had to have some slight list for that it would not drag the ground. It was the same now, when she finally freed himself from his statue resembled position and slowly started walking towards the entrance at number 119. It sought the name of the orange-painted vestibule was also there on the board. However, under the heading "3 steps". Consolation was anyway, the apartment was second from the top. Despite this, she dragged both bag and himself up the steep and narrow stairs. The name on the door was identical with that of the second part of the torn note. She rang the bell and waited. The stairwell was barren and inhospitable. Each step echoed between the stairs and the walls. At the top was, however, a window that let in some natural light. But barely reached down to the ground floor. Called on again ... but no one opened. Was perhaps too much to ask that people would be at home. Especially for just the day she intended to make a visit. Just lugging everything down again. If only it was an elevator, she thought.While she was on the way down distractedly read the different names of the apartment doors. Many who she neither heard nor seen before. Apparently it can be named anything, she thought in amazement.

The growing hunger led her back to the cafe with the men outside. They were still there and now additionally loudly discussing. Probably something private and for the day very important topic. Hardly any solution on the life of the streets. She could easily hear. Self she sat inside the cafe. Ordered the green tea and something to eat. Counted out the money again. Stated that she was still relatively in funds. Something that probably would not last forever. But she had not come here, to worry about the future. But instead of living in the moment and able to enjoy their freedom. Although she would have to just live for the day. For her life already had too long been too structured. That was why she was now sitting here. In a cafe somewhere in the great city of southern China. Admittedly a little worried but most uplifting and almost euphoric by the mere thought.

Asked a girl in the staff, if any possibly recognized the name Chen Chiu. Thus a man who would stay in the house no. 119 next door. She shook though her head. They only know people to look here, she explained. Know almost never what they called. Yin is my name, she said, bowing slightly. Got however, only a forced smile back. Without any name came from her lips. Perhaps it is in this city, that would be a bit more anonymous. Do not let people get too close in on life, she thought, and slurped a little distracted in their tea. All the while she was watching the street life in and outside the cafe. Keep in mind that nobody here knows who I am and where I come from. Not a clue where I was and what I did yesterday. Actually feels quite nice in any way. That nobody cares, that is. Actually she does not either if truth be told. Was in fact not that kind of man. Probably one of the reasons she chose Guangzhou ...!?

Chen Chiu was obviously not therefore her grandmother. Nevertheless her uncle. He did not have much contact with the rest of the family now. Not since Yin's mother, that Chen's sister, remarried with the stepfather.Almost the only thing she knew about Uncle Chen was that he worked as a foreman at a factory in Guangzhou. It was with him that now the hopes and expectations low. If she begged and begged, maybe he could accommodate her for a while. To begin with, anyway. Moreover, he had perhaps some contacts in the city? Which would then facilitate the ability to find a job. So she had anyway imagined it all. It would still not go, she'll try to find another solution. For back home to the country ... that option was no longer in her thinking.

Amidst speculations came a younger man in torn jeans and a cigarette in his mouth over to her table. He had been sitting together with some other guys at a table farther away. Without introducing himself, he said ...

- Do you want to buy a mobile phone?
- No, I have no phone.
- But look here! It is a brand new Samsung. The worst kind! Costs safe two thousand yuan. New words! You get it for ... five hundred. A bargain that is.
- No, I do not even have that much money, tried to Yin, that he would leave.
- Jaman ... OK ... say three hundred then ..!? It's really cheap for this. A smartphone that is. You see ... a new smartphone for a femhundring!
- You said three hundred recently retorted Yin instinctively and quickly as a cobra, but changed his mind at the moment. Would the definitely have no phone ... at all.
- Yes, yes ... you get the well for three hundred then. I am not so greedy.
- As I said, I shall have no telephone. Do not you see, she said, and started to get annoyed.
- It is quiet girl. Have a great day! Cool bag by the way ...

Yin looked long away toward the table where the whole gang kid sat and chatted. Sometimes laughter spirit to something wittily as someone said. Wondered what that was for a collection of shady types, however. Certainly, no serious-working guys.

After a good hour at the diner began wood flavor make itself felt. Rose therefore and paid. Fresh air again. Stood for a moment, watching the street life outside. Tried to get an idea of how the people here really dressed.Which hairstyles and what they had on their feet. Thought it was interesting. But as time went on, the more miserable she looked, she thought. Her thin white linen, and these old worn pants. Only surprising that more looking at me, she thought. But the people did not seem to care. It was just to thank and receive. In the end, dragging her back to the house number 119 on Kengkou Rd. . Sat down outside the entrance. Use the bag as a kind of chair with the house wall as a backrest. Began to feel tired and almost sleepy. Street background noise became like a lullaby, where the thoughts of all that happened during the day was played back in her head. I felt so unreal it all. Maybe it's just a dream, she thought. Once you wake up at home in bed ...!?

Woke up she did, however, also, but now the sound of something rattled. Looked up and saw a smiling elderly little wrinkled lady with a shopping cart. Yin found himself rapidly. Asked if she felt Chen Chiu. And so, when he used to come home on the day.

- Oh, Mr Chiu. Well, I think that he usually come home shortly after six. However, he does not every day. I know that.
- Well, because I'm waiting for him, namely.
- Well ... joo as I said ... I see him often get home at that time. Lives namely at the bottom of this house. Behind that window. Are you his daughter perhaps?
- No, I'm ... he is ... my uncle actually.
- Well ... joo as I said ... oh well, yes but ... then you may well wait for him inside of me. Can sit by the window so you can see when he comes. Nice not having to wait out here.
- Thanks! That was nice.

Yin positioned itself strategically right by the window inside the old woman. With perfect views towards the entrance. The unusually friendly white-haired lady then did prepare some tea for them both. Then sat himself opposite Yin. In its floral blue and white dress with matching white pearl necklace. Slurped noisily from his big cup and appeared at the same time enjoy the steaming beverage. Apparently, she had been out shopping food.Despite the invigorating tea, she seemed a little tired. Talked yet with Yin about everything. Also smiled like that pillimariskt all the time. Was apparently quite curious by itself. Yin did not disclose the actual reason for his visit. But thought the lady was both funny and cute in any way. Actually, long ago, she laughed so much. They fit well together despite the age difference. Minutes were soon to an hour and Yin also had time to taste her freshly baked cake. Said it was delicious but did not dare to ask for a piece of. But as always when you're having fun, it will be interrupted. This time, however, because of a pleasanter reason. Her uncle, Chen was seen suddenly headed for the house. Yin stood up and thanked the lady with a quick hug. Took his bag and went out into the stairwell. Met him with a big smile ...

- Hello! Do not you recognize me?
- Aaah ... I should perhaps it ... ??
- But ... it's me ... Yin ...
- Yin !? What? Is it really you? Is there anything that has happened ... or?
- Well, nothing special ... Well, that is ... I'm here now ... all by myself. Without the mother and the others. I have left everything!
- Well, it was really a surprise. Yin! What big you have become ... and ... cute too.

It was not long until they sat up in his apartment. She finally got to tell his whole story. He listened with interest and wide-eyed. Nodded also understanding all the

time. Opened a beer and asked if she wanted ... before
the food. Yin thanked surprised myself yes. They
clinked glasses and he greeted her welcome. Had never
drunk a whole bottle of beer brand yourself, but
thought ... this is of course my new life now. So why
not.

- Do you think I can stay here for a while? Until I find a
job that is.
- Well, it'll go well. For a while, anyway. In this case, you
take the little room, he said, pointing toward a
door. Has the most offices. Is actually a bed there too.
- Thanks! It's very kind of you, if I get it. I had to come
in to the lady at the bottom, while I waited for you. She
was so cute and kind.
- Well, that is old woman Wang. She knows everyone in
this house. Is a bit of a godmother for us. Well just
that. It was one thing I thought of. It may even can be a
vacancy at the factory. Where I work, that is. Do namely
that it is now lacking ironing staff there.
- Ironing employees !? What is it?
- Well, we manufacture the jeans where and when they
are finished, they have ironed and pressed. With iron
that is.
- Aha ...!?!
- I'll hear them tomorrow, so we'll see. It's a pretty good
job. At least in comparison with all the others there. But

you must reckon with overtime sometimes ... unfortunately.

She sat long in bed that night, and flipping through some of Uncle Chen's magazines. A whole pile to him by the girls at the factory. He said anyway. Thought it was so interesting with all these pictures of famous people.Not that she knew so many of them, but still. Felt in any way complicit. For now, she was the last of the big city. And it was here that life itself was. At least what she imagined and still innocently imagined. Now there in bed half reclining with a big comfy pillow under his head. Chen had already left the apartment and therefore she was alone at home. Despite the darkness settled over the city, she felt quite at ease anyway. And why not ?!An entire apartment in Guangzhou for itself. Who would have dreamed about it for just a few days ago.

Suddenly she remembered. Stood up and stuck tentative hand into her tight trouser pocket. Hauled up a gold necklace with some sparkling stones hanging in the middle. This is certainly the gold, she thought somewhat excited. At the same time as her conscience began to crack. What had she done ... really? Did it just for yourself. It just happened. The necklace lay there. So irresistibly to himself in the bowl on the hall Agency. Himself had never taken such a fine piece of jewelry. However, began to repent. Would she return it? No, it did not feel good either. Then it would all things are revealed and what would happen. Comforted however, that the old woman Wang would probably assume that she mislaid it somewhere. So she understood think. Certainly, she would surely look for it. But could never prove that someone really taken it. Upholstered therefore down collar in the suitcase and then proceeded blithely their mental dream journey into the world of celebrity magazines. Until she fell asleep exhausted on the bed. With the newspaper on his chest and with his clothes still on.

Woke up it was light in the room. Looked at the clock as already become half past eight. Even so, she felt tough and tired. Pushed aside the blanket from the bed warm body. Was met instead by the cool air in the room.Rubbed his sleepy tired eyes. Aside from some noise from the street outside, everything was quiet and still. Uncle Chen is of course a long time ago at work, she thought. Closed his eyes and remained a while longer. Let the soul slowly preparing for the new day. Eventually, however, began the hunger to make itself felt. Was not in the habit to sleep so long. Unless she had the night shift in the drying house, of course. Eventually hunger and impatience too great. Jumped out of bed with a leap. Went out to the kitchen for some breakfast. It, like Chen already had prepared the night before. On the stove was a pot of

Jook. A kind of hot rice gruel that most reminded por-
ridge. The gas stove was of the same type at home, so
the breakfast was soon on the table. Along with bread, a
little jam and even a cup of green tea. After a half hour
at the kitchen table and a quick shower, she was ready
for the day's exercises in the big city. Took out a new
panty from the suitcase and even switched his sweaty
tank top against a pink t-shirt. While the hair dried, she
stood for a long while at the window. Watched the
world go down the street. At the same time tightly
clutching their newly acquired apartment key. Almost as
if someone might take it away from her. On the other
side of the street, she saw a woman with a hood and a
long brush with red handle. Seemed to work with to
brush and clean the sidewalk. A fruit vendor near un-
packed their boxes. Overflowing with colorful and refreshing fruits. Next to the fruit stall was a newsstand. Where some young men apparently stood and
free read ...!? Yin opened the window a crack and immediately felt the stench of smog. On her familiar odor
that was as common in Hengyang. The sounds of a
truck and a hot-tempered scooter pressed arbitrarily set
by fönsterglipan. In addition to the usual cycle appeared
just these vehicles being the most common in Guangzhou's street scene. She had already noticed.

The feeling of freedom was tremendous, when she for
the first time alone wandering the street. Tossed casually

with her hair in the balmy breeze. Let the city cherish her in her womb. Had in any obvious way already become a part of it. All that she had so long yearned. This was now lying at her feet. At the disposal of those who wanted and had the courage to take for themselves. And it was really her. Be prepared to sacrifice everything.In order to fully live out the dream. Whoever in the drying house for a long time been founded. All that could now be realized. Of her, totally self besides. No longer chanted and steered. No longer stuck in the structured life from the beginning mapped out for her. Felt his eyes moistened. Not of sorrow but just the feeling to be so divinely fulfilled by anything. What did she really not. But it did not matter. For now she was there. After far too heavy years in dödskuggans country, she had risen again. As a newly sprung sunflower swaying in the wind she went weightless along the paved promenade. And even smiled at a police officer in his light blue shirt and peaked cap. Suddenly felt the woman awake in himself. Also found all the young couples that went hand in hand. What were the thirst for love that almost burst the heart. Now understood what she had missed. And what lack done with her. Was nonetheless grateful to himself for his inner strength. The force that led her to let go. Forced her to come out of the darkness. In order to follow the star that long shone so strongly.

Outside a flower shop stood a few fruit cartons of fresh chicken eggs. Right next to them a few water-filled tubs with orange fish swimming around in circles. If the possibility existed, she would have taken up the fishermen and threw them into the sea. Knew how it felt to be trapped. Imagine just being able to swim around and around in a bowl. All the while life so seductive shimmer wherever outside. On the sidewalk, like a hole in the wall, was a small shop that sold grilled lizard-breakers. What lay there gleaming maroon and symmetrically lined up on a plate. Yin did not feel immediately attracted by the sight. In addition, she was still measured after breakfast. But most of it was so new to her. Everything possible that surprised all the time. Really enjoyed the news, and diversity. Of all the new sensations that constantly insisted on her attention. I will never get tired of this, she thought.

A few blocks later she saw a small dog. The cute little fellow was owned probably by an elderly uncle who was sitting at one of the tables. Namely, a newspaper wrinkled tanned gentleman there on the outdoor terrace.Instead called Chawan and looked most like a better cafe, you could say. Yin could not resist the temptation but stopped, to get acquainted with the dog. It had quite short hair was dark brown in color and had ears that stood straight up. Reminded actually a rävunge. She looked up at the man behind the newspaper and said timidly ...

- Ooohh, what is the cute. What's that?
- Oh, you mean doggy !? Thought for a while that you were talking about me ...!?
- Ha ha ha ... No, but it sure is nice ... so incredibly sweet.
- Joo, it is called Yang. It is a mongrel dog. A cross between a Pomeranian and yes ... something else. I really do not know what. Has incidentally just turned one year.
- Yeah. Well, one of those I would also like to have.

Said Yin with a kind of praying tone. While she tenderly stroked it. It was a long-repressed desire for a dog now got her feelings to wake up. Had often wished for a but always been denied by the stepfather. On the grounds that "it's just useless wretch who are always in the way." However, could never accept his cruel attitude to these wonderful creatures. Had finally tired of his own nagging and reluctantly reconciled to the reality. Simply nipped physical longing for a dog. A friend that she could play and cuddle with. For example, when life often had an ability to get too lonely and difficult.

- You are welcome to meet him again. I sit most of the time here with the newspaper and take a cup. I almost

live here, you might say. It would in any case staff say, if you asked them.
- Thanks! That I really want. Or how Yang? Sure you want it?

She said, and lifted him up in the front feet. All the while the man smiled and squinted his narrow eyes over reading glasses. Yin managed, however reluctantly, to tear themselves away from the dog and left Chawan in a dream-like state. A dog ..! Imagine having your own dog. Continued their stroll and explore the streets. Saw some Buddhist monks in orange clothes that settled down in a small green park. Everyone sat on the same kind of pallets. Namely made of orange plastic with four legs. Then, in the same color as their long coats. The type of pallets she had seen before. Actually a bit of everything during his so far short city tour. Just wondered what was special about them? Further down the street, she discovered a glass booth. Raised a few yuan from the wallet and bought a ginseng ice cream. One of her familiar kind previously. In addition, one of the favorites. The little kiosk was in front of a low stone wall bordering a green area. Sat down there on the wall with his legs dangling freely. While the rapidly melting ice cream with pleasure was enjoyed. All the while she studied folk life and other interesting things that happened round about.

Now mother would see me, she thought. Sitting here all alone down in Guangzhou. Licking on a big ice cream. Moreover bought for her savings, it hit her simultaneously. The ice cream suddenly had a bitter aftertaste. Even mixed with the occasional salty tear found its way down to the mouth. Was actually a bit melancholic and slightly remorseful. Could not help but think of those back home. Will everything on the farm continue without me, she thought, and licked up with a little melted ice cream that flowed down along the cone. Felt as if she had taken anything away from them. Certainly nothing that was their property, yet something always belonged to them.Which has been part of the farm and the life there. And my brother ... what is he doing now? Certainly yes, he's in school, of course. And no longer helping him with homework. I wonder who he plays with in the evenings?Well, issues jostling with each other. But the answers floating unanswered remain within her. They're probably wondering where I am and what I do. Maybe even if I'm still alive ...!? All that actually had not beaten her until now. So there would be. What if they even been out looking for me, she thought troubled. Imagine ...!? Maybe the mom is not even found the flower in the casket yet !? In contrast to the bike no longer there at home, they should already have been discovered.

It had already become afternoon, when she reluctantly looked back toward Nr.119 Kengkou Rd. Before that, even had a lunch in the form of spring roll and noodle soup been enjoyed. In a simple but nice serving. Once at the house felt again the need for sleep to come over her. Maybe it was the new environment. Luckily, she did not see the old lady Wang. When she tired but satisfied Segade up the stairs to the apartment. Searched in the refrigerator for something to quench your thirst with. Surprised, she found instead a huge stock of beer cans in one of the downstairs kitchen cabinets. Had never seen so many beers in one place. Everyone was off the mark Tsingta. Thought that if only one of them disappears, so noticeable, it probably is not. Therefore opened a jar and greeted half right on the spot. With the can in his hand was occupied since the already ingrained position in bed. Half lying on the large pillow with a weekly newspaper on the stomach. Soon, deep in the fashion and celebrity world glittering dreamland. A world that so long waited for her. At last she was there and the door was already wide open. Anytime she would unmarked able to slip into. Was very fascinated by the famous fashion photographer Chen Man cool pictures. A woman who truly had its own expression in photography. She was not alone to enjoy. Even the Japanese Manga look with her large eyes she appreciated.

After a while she felt a bit drowsy. Yes almost giddy even. Belched high and uninhibited. The carbon dioxide and the alcohol had obviously done his. For shortly after that she began to laugh out loud. Probably just about something trivial in the newspaper that suddenly appeared comical. Lightly salon intoxicated, you could say. Though it did not herself. Had no experience at all of the so-called strong drinks. It as been at home, was usually some kind of spirits in bottles stepfather had full control. No one dared touch them. Especially not when he was drunk.

The door to her room stood wide open, when Uncle Chen came home at seven o'clock in the evening. He looked in and saw Yin flat on the bed. Sleeping with a beer in hand and a pile of newspapers beside.

- Hello there! How is it? Have you been like that all night, he shouted jokingly.
- Huh ...!? No, I took a can of beer in the cabinet, mumbled Yin RENASCENT staring surprised back. Was so thirsty after my walk around town. But you'll get paid. Never mind.
- Oh, you like beer then !?
- No, but I just found nothing drinkable.
- It is quiet. I've got enough. Thought cook a fish soup now, if you feel hungry.
- Well happy! Thanks!

- But tomorrow, you tighten up. Have namely whacked a job for you at the factory. That which I mentioned yesterday. Ironing words. Then you have to get up already at five, half past five. We start namely six thirty. It is there in time, if you go from here about ten past six.

Yin sat up in bed but did not quite. She would start work the next day? Smiled a little naive surprise to him. While some concerns drew his shadow over her. Was further told that the salary paid fortnightly. And that, as previously said, sometimes have to work overtime on some evenings. Not first week as an apprentice, explained Chen in an attempt to be persuasive.

She helped to set the table for dinner. Took out a beer to Chen, but contented himself with a glass of cold green tea from yesterday. Did not think she was feeling so good after the beer. Is probably not for me, she thought, while they slowly savored the hot spiced and hot soup. Along with a freshly baked white bread Chen bought on the way home. Afterward they sat at the table for a long while and talked. Much about her future job and life itself in the factory. About the camaraderie that also was there. Everything that she would be as prepared as possible.

The total degradation

It was early morning and still almost dark, when Yin and her uncle went away from home. Night fog was still like a wet cap over the streets. A smell of burnt coal mixed with fog. Unfortunately, nothing unusual for a city in southern China at this time of year. Normally used Chen bike to work, but today he led his side. After a fifteen minute walk strode onto the factory site. China South Garments said a big sign above the entrance. First passed a sentry box where a striped boom was lowered over the entrance. After the ID-checking took the then stairs up to the second floor. To the plane of denim manufacturing. Namely, where Yin from today would work.Furthermore, through a doorway where thick plastic strips hanging down. However, only after a truck passing through the shredded door. She was not at all prepared for the noise inside the premises. It was even forced to raise his voice, to be able to talk to each other. The sound from all textile machines together became a rhythmic melody that filled the whole room. They went to another room, where the noise was slightly lower. But still enough because of all the sewing machines that went at full speed. When the machines sat most young girls with white caps. Fully occupied with twisting and turning of fabric pieces and then sewn together.

Yin almost got weak in the knees, by what she saw. That they could do all that ...?! And so quickly at that. Luckily it did not get one of those jobs, she thought. Just as Chen paused at the door to a square small office in the middle of the room. The upper half of the walls were made of glass. So you could see both in and out. Where she presented for her future boss, Mr. Ma. A definite and accurate balding man in his fifties. When Chen then went back to his own job as a foreman in the washing department, Mr Ma took her on a quick tour of the factory. First up to a warehouse where large bales of raw cotton were in long rows on the floor. Here it is in any case relatively quiet for a change, she managed just think, before they came into the mill. Where large machinery was working to make thread of cotton. But with significantly fewer employees. From the mill went thread to no color. Some of them were allowed to keep their white color, while most were blue.

The spun and dyed thread transported to the weaving. Where were the denim fabric for jeans. After it was passed to cut and soon they were back in the sewing workshop. On all these chewing sewing machines and the hard-working girls who sewed the pants. Yin noticed that it stood JUKI on the side of all the sewing machines. What it stood for, she did not. Maybe it was just a business name ..!?

The legs of the ready-made jeans then blown up that long balloons. All of that could more easily brush them. One use hard brushes, because they would have a more worn patina. See some more use out simply. From the treatment was running out into the wash. Where they are in large barrels were rolled around in the water with volcanic stones. After the last item on the tour they arrived at Yin's work. At the deletion thus. With iron in their hands, they saw to it that the jeans had a smoother surface without any folds. Mr Ma also told us that a pair of jeans in total took 15 minutes to produce. How to really counted, did not understand the Yin. But nodded and at least looked impressed out. The first week she would go as an apprentice. Therefore presented the prospective colleagues for her by Mr Ma. Also found out lunch times and other practical before she was handed over to the department. First day of her first re-al job had begun.

Time passed and soon the first week past. The days seemed long and the heat in the factory did, you felt completely exhausted in the evenings. Even so, it was her newfound colleagues who got her motivated to drag himself back there each morning. Most of them lived in dorms that were directly adjacent to the factory. Yin had received follow up to the rooms sometimes at lunch time and there was no place she would thrive on. Not too many square inches for itself. Admittedly, they had each other to socialize with. But even that could be too much of. Therefore, she felt happy, to live in an ordinary apartment. Went happy that walk every day to avoid the dorms.At home, one can take a shower, eat and sleep, just when you want to, she realized.

First free weekend day, she and some mates metro into the Zhujiang - New Town. To Shang Xia Jiu or Beijing Road as the most developed. There are shopping street, number one in Guangzhou. There, they really liked everybody. Getting goes around there in the crowds and look at all the excitement. To say nothing of the large supply. All enticing goods inside the stores. Clothing, jewelry and above all perfumes. Obviously, they had to take advantage of all the free samples offered. Therefore, soon left all a long tail scent of French perfume behind. All the while giggling go between the shops along the street. They experienced some relaxing and enjoyable moments together. Without having to think about the factory and the tedious jobs. Just get to enjoy life. They also had time to satisfy its hunger on a Dakasi bar. Before a long evening walk along the Zhujiang River and Haiyin Bridge began. The river also known as the Pearl River, meanders so beautifully through the city. For next Sunday, they decided to visit the great grand department store China Plaza. An eight-storey great palace where most are. If time was sufficient, they would also visit Liwan. The old city.

After another week of wear at the factory, she got her first paycheck. 1260 yuan, after tax. For two weeks of work, that is. However, even without any overtime fortunately. When she came home that night, Chen was already at home in the apartment. He and some loud mates sitting in the kitchen and talked. Played cards and drank beer. Cheered dutifully at them before she went into her room. After paying Chen a symbolic sum for the rent of the room, it was still a good penny over. She had just figured out. In the bed where she sat and calculated on the debit and credit. With both honorable and dishonorable earned money. Musing dreamily at everything one could buy. This city is the most one can wish for, she had noticed. Though it is clear, you do not need to pay for absolutely everything. She convinced herself with and picked up a small white cardboard from the fabric bag. With the text "Elizabeth Arden" surface ...!? Opened the lid slightly excited and hauled up a small wonderfully beautiful bottle. It was almost heart-shaped the checkered glass with polished metal around. The lid was like a small glass orbs in the same grid and the metal became "UNTOLD". A perfume spray. Took off the lid and put the bottle to his nose. Felt a strong and tantalizing aromatic scent. First did not want to waste the content of the precious drops. But could not resist the temptation and gave himself a couple of short puffs behind the ears. Just like movie stars did. Went around the room for a moment and let themselves be seduced by the aromatic experience. Felt again feminine in any way. Although the smell was not on par with her other revelation. Such as unwashed hair, dirty jeans and a cheap cotton swab. Her self-image was hanging safely together with her age.And the habit at all new alien worldly things that she was forced to relate to. When and how this perfume got into her bag, just knew herself. For none of the other girls neither saw nor knew anything. Did not show the perfume for them. Knew of course that it was wrong. Yes, even illegally, of course. But considered himself still does not like a thief. Could sometimes just can not resist the temptation. It was that simple. While she felt elated by it all. Got a kick out simply. Afterwards, she could certainly experience a certain remorse. But the repressed rather quickly. The rest of the evening was the tiredness increasingly apparent. The adventures out on the town was more challenging than you might think. Undressed and went to bed. Looked a little distracted in the old newspapers before she fell asleep. Still exotically fragrant and with the old lady's gold necklace around his neck.

Throughout the week, she occasionally appreciative praise for the fine necklace. Many wondered where she bought it. The explanation was that she inherited it from her grandmother, who died a few years ago. So believable that she almost believed in it. Anyone who does not at all asked about the necklace, was the only guy on the deletion. A rather shy boy who most looked at her on the sly. Always struck down his eyes when Yin happened to look at him. Almost thought he was a little in love with her !? However, Yin was also shy of the opposite sex, and why it happened often nothing more. At lunchtime he sat Moreover together with the other guys. Thought, however at him sometimes in the evenings in solitude. Something special is still with him, she thought. Almost had the same feeling as the first time she saw Jianyu from the neighboring farm. Tomorrow I'll take on me that perfume and a little lipstick, she thought. Then I ask him if anything about the job itself. Anything. It does not matter. Only it does not seem all too transparent. Smiled to himself while the steam from the iron more heat into her red cheeks.

It then became long weeks on the job. Must namely often work several hours of overtime. Luckily, they got the opportunity, to get a bite to eat before the evening session. But until the wee hours felt fatigue and futility of ever more palpable. Sweating profusely in the heat while the right arm increasingly tightened and ached. Took the opportunity often to drink half a bottle of water while rapidly rag in the face of the toilet. For managers were namely the bite. As soon as someone seemed to bind or rest for long, so they arrived. It was, among other things, what made the work so stressful and monotonous, she thought. If any manager criticized the length of her pauses, they were often angry and arrogant response back. In the style of ... "then we may well change jobs, you and I" ...!?

Was alerted that there still shone at the lady on the ground floor. Despite the late hour when she finally came home after a long day's work. Walked with heavy steps up the stairs and put the key in the lock. Already outside the door was heard loud voices inside the apartment. It proved to be Chen's friends who was there again. As usual, busy with their discussions. Slurring and gesticulating there around the kitchen table. Which also, as usual, was full of empty beer cans. Some had not even got a place but lay scattered around on the floor. They are not exaggerating if we say that the right was not something nonconformist meeting that took place there. Yin felt uncomfortable with their presence. Therefore closed the door unnoticed, and disappeared into his room. They were even too påstrukna to even notice her. Had bought with him a box with stir-fried meat and rice from the snack bar on the way home. Hungry as she was after the day's hard toil. Did not want to go into the kitchen and get some sticks, but used instead a fork that still lay unwashed earlier. An hour after supper, she made up for with clean comfy sheets. Crouched down and fell asleep immediately despite the noise outside.

For some reason she woke up. Everything was so quiet and still. But still felt the feeling that something was not as it should. Still only half awake, she seemed to sense a flash of light from the door. At the same time the feeling that the blanket was missing. Stretched eyes shut out his arm to re pull it over itself. It was then that all hell broke out !! Her arm was pressed against the bed. Suddenly she felt that someone sat on her. Immediately understood that it was a man. And also had time to think, that it should be one of Chen's friends. In the backlight from the door you could not see what he looked like. But spirits scent of the heavy breaths was all the more palpable. You're my own little concubine, he moaned excitedly and tore her panties with one hand. Yin then tried to turn himself free. Also knew that the man was completely naked. Was completely panicked and screamed.Chen Chen ... ... she cried. Help! Immediately received a slap across the face. Of which she immediately fell silent. However, most of just shock. Is not still, I beat you again, you bitch, he said and spread her legs. You are my horse and I ride you, when I want. Just when I want! Do you get it ?! The thoughts bounced around desperately in Yin's head. He will kill me, or ...?!?

Knew how he and penetrated her. How all his heavy body rhythmically began to swing towards her. How she wanted to scream with pain and anguish, she remained silent. Seconds felt like minutes and the only sound was his moaning and bed creaking. During a brief moment brightened her thoughts. I must do something, she realized more and more desperate. Reached out one hand towards the bedside table and trying to reach the lamp there.But it was too far away. Instead, she felt the cardboard box from the snack bar with her hand while also fork which remained there. Groped and struggled desperately to get a grip on it. Which with the help of higher powers to end successfully. Noticed at the same time how he increased the pace of her rocking on her. Jewels therefore all possible force that the abundant flow of adrenaline provided her with ... and stabbed to. Did some quick shock before he became too stiff body. Uttered some sort of gurgling groan and then fell heavily together just limp over her. Heard his sighing exhale directly into the ear. Unfortunately also the disgusting liquor smell from the mouth. With plenty of power completely threw her over him on the side and was able to break free. He rolled However, immediately back on the belly. Once up out of bed, she tried in panic to locate their clothes. Just before the room was left, she threw a quick glance back toward the bed. The last image that nailed themselves to the retina showed a naked, white and hairy man's body. Lying on his stomach with a fork standing straight up from the buttocks. Before the escape down the stairs, she noted, that the apartment incidentally seemed to be completely empty. Not a soul in sight.

Ran along the darkened and almost deserted street. Until she could not cope any longer. Stayed panting up at a lighted street corner to catch his breath. Looked really nothing of the surroundings. For her entire head was a single fusion of thoughts and feelings. String of anxiety that desperately crowded with memories from home. However, became aware of a cold and wet feeling on the inside of the thighs. Undid the button of his trousers.Upholstered hand down to feel for. On which she then looked for a long while. Some kind of messy with red streaks in. Felt very disgusting and uncomfortable. Realizing that the red probably have to be blood. She guessed anyway. Perhaps all the rest Scary from the wound where the fork penetrated, she thought uneasily. Perhaps I have even killed him? What should I do ...?

Dried of the most kletet on the hand against a wall. It is between the legs with a paper handkerchief which thankfully was in his pocket. Got retching by just the sight. Spat also reflexively all the time. As if she wants to get out to something distasteful. Only when the worst disgust emotions subsided, she felt pain in the abdomen. As an aching wound. A chafing sense that made her go straddle, when she confused then continued down the street. The night felt slightly cool. But had still had presence in the moment to put on a sweater before the apartment was left. Slipper anyway to freeze, she sighed and sat down on the stone floor in a port rise. Crouched against the wall with his head resting in his hands. Wanted to shield themselves of external reality. In trying to console itself. An illusory comfort that still could not stop the tears from flowing down his cheeks. Now understood that she was in trouble. Whatever the future.

With stiff and frozen body after some half-sleeping hours in port, she found an open bar. There was already a couple explicit newly awakened men and took their early breakfast. Self she ordered green tea and ostsandwich. Sat in the only soft comfortable sofa that was there. With teacup light shaking of the hand was taken to the steaming hot beverage during noisily slurping. Was still too tired to take in, what happened to her during the night. Could now only live in the present. Probably a natural reaction of brain displacement mechanism. The lack of sleep caused her to spend some additional hours in that couch. Recumbent with open mouth and eyes closed.Blithely oblivious to all the customers who came and went during the period. Luckily, no one had time to even care about her. Everyone had their thinking about. Even the staff was more than fully occupied with serving their risers customers.

Before the bar was left at half eight o'clock, she consulted a younger guy on the staff. If he possibly knew some who rented out rooms. For after much deliberation, she decided to leave Chen's bunk. The apartment was now associated with such large negative emotions. Moreover, she knew not, what happened to that man. Or creature rather. Could be seriously injured or even dead, she thought. Knew all too well what happens to that killing another person. In the worst cases, death. For how would she be able to prove, what the devil did to her? Probably not at all. So the risk she would absolutely not take. A longer life than this, she had actually intended. After asking a colleague among the staff, he came with a vague hand-written note with directions. This is some kind of office that deals with rental and also selling homes, he said. Thanked for enlightenment and reluctantly left the heat in the bar. Gave then off as described. The tragic and obvious reasons now slightly wider apart than normal.

<u>Alone is strongest</u>

Already after a few hours she put the key in the lock. The door that from now went to her new home. A room with a kitchenette and toilet in the corridor. Actually, just a couple blocks from the street where Chen was staying. Must pay an advance on the rent but felt nevertheless quite happy. Had in any case nowhere to go in the middle of all the sad misery. The room was the easiest conceivable. In a big way just a bed with table, chair and chair. On the walls a bright worn wallpaper which one wall adorned with a dark dog racing. Pretty well matching the ugly bedside lamp additionally. The room's only window faced a dark and narrow courtyard. Most just a brown wall that view. Consolation of the window was all the same, that the room could at least be aired. A kitchenette with gas plate and small sink just to the left inside the door. Unfortunately no refrigerator, she noted little disappointed in the rapidly completed the inspection. Took off his sweaty shoes. Went out to the shower room in the hallway and took a long shower. Felt dirty inside and outboard. Wanted to wash away the thoughts and the polluted feeling that existed everywhere. Forget all as soon as possible. If now it could ?! Luckily included both sheets and towels in the rent. After being dried up and the wet hair, she threw herself down on the bed. Immediately saw a spider perched in one corner. But could not seem to care. What is a spider against everything else that happened? It still can not get much worse, she thought. Eyes shut for a moment, thinking.Finally arrived at ... to go back to work at the factory was not to think about. Did not even meet with Chen again Especially not after what his friend did. Could not forgive that they could leave it there full pig in the apartment. Alone with her in addition !? What it came to work at the factory, she had already tired. Being trapped there all day ... no thanks. Toil like a slave ... never. Just work, eat and sleep. What was life? No, anything but more of that. It was quite clear.

A few hours later at the station Kengkou she was already on his way down to the subway. Hopefully a cooler place than up there in the street quivering heat. Now on their way to the big department store China Plaza. Must forget everything, she thought! And there instead take part of the diversity and luxury. The mall, which she and her comrades from the factory still thought to visit for the weekend. Did not really have anything else to think about. A facile way but still an attempt to console himself. Now, in the solitude of the thoughts of all that afflicted her. Most of all she missed her mother. Especially her good food. In the absence of that she thought acquire some food to his new lair on

the way home. Must might still survive ... despite everything.

Got on the subway line 1 and sat alone on a 4-seat
space. A few stations later storms three girls in the
20-year-age into the cart. Put on the vacant seats beside
her. At first she thought that it felt good to have some
company. Especially in the rather insecure environment
like a subway car often represents. At least for a sole
and lately also rape girl. However, this was no ordinary
girls. It was like a whole new universe suddenly opened
and filled the whole room around her. In addition to the
chewing gum constantly and talking at each other, so
they hung where angry white in-ear headphones down
from the ears. Obviously ended in a respective mobile
phone of cutting. While the mouths incessantly walked
on them, everyone sat and wrote feverishly on where
their SMS. Despite its silver-painted and impractical
long nails. All this while they discussed the music that
everyone listened to. They also showed each other pictures of themselves in the mobiles. Cheerfully and loudly commenting them. One of the girls also managed to
keep a mirror in his hand, while the lip gloss was im-
proved a bit. It could, God forbid, has been too little of
that good ..!?

One of the girls were attentive to Yin's wide-eyed and
astonished gaze. Perhaps it was her expression slightly

very full of inferiority and jealousy. And the girl who probably noted it immediately began to look for something in her purse. However, it would only prove that she probably felt too over stimulated ... after all !? For out of the bag hauled a tablet. All showed something that apparently her mother (?!) sent. What other girlfriends commented cheerfully. While text-writing meanwhile progressed with the same intensity. Then said some of the girls, the music in her headphones currently not sufficiently stimulating. Wanted to be listened in one of the others also lurks. So after she sat then with a hook from the respective mobile ears. That stereo does not seem so important now ... obviously !? Yin was so fascinated by the whole theater piece that was played live in front of her. Heard therefore nothing, what they are really talking about. But, no, it was the world's problems was discussed. Probably something far more locally if you say so. However, managed to Yin heard that someone said ... "... and then he kissed me" ...!? Probably it was well at that level that the conversation took place !? It is well accepted that women have better human multitasking than men. And maybe ... was this event the most tangible proof of the theory.

Yin's initial admiration turned more and more to hate. Especially when they whisper to each other disparaging looked at her old clothes and shoes. She understood very well what it was all about. However, they were soon in front of the Lie Shi Ling Yaan. Or Martyrs Park station in China Plaza also called. It turned out that even the poppy girl gang would get off there. Therefore they stood all of the doors and waited. While Yin himself was right behind them. Enviously studied their elegant dress, shoes and accessories. Just when the doors opened, she suddenly see a tablet sticking out of one girl's satchel. In the crush that occurred when everyone would leave the carriage, stretched Yin just out his hand and took it. Simply ... just like that! Before she knew it, she stood there on the platform with a tablet in his hand. All the while the girl gang unsuspecting disappeared into the crowd.Found, however, quickly and stuffed it inside the waistband. That is, the half that had place. The rest she covered with a shirt. The zipper quickly pulled back. Took the precaution remained downstairs in the station for a while. Before she eventually decided to take the escalator up to the big department store. Palace on 3 Zhongshan Street. Namely the mall.

Barely had time to get into the store until a skating rink suddenly appeared. Full of people of all ages who almost weightless gliding across the ice to nice background music. Had never seen anything like that in reality. Just stood and gaped. Admiring, but mostly surprised that it was even possible ...!? Also noticed that many off the track went around with something that appeared to be coffee mugs. Actually, she drank herself never or rarely coffee. But still took courage and asked a couple of girls, where they had bought the coffee. Thinking that she would not be worse than them. Ten minutes later she also heard the same javaläppjande crowd. Stood at the rink boards and slurped out of the hot, freshly brewed beverage. Not at all so stupid, she thought. At least with a little sugar in. Felt already part of that life. Namely, life in the city. There she had so long dreamed of. But on the other hand, skating ... that she was not going to try on.

Instead, she went further up the escalator through the department store's glittering floor. Almost became confused by all the business' Western signs such as Esprit, HM, Lacoste, Levis, Mango, Adidas, American Express, McDonalds and 7eleven. Samsung knew she certainly recognized from television'n home. But what played the sign 'names really matter. It was the stores themselves that it was essential. And they completely pulled her to him. It was really needed no barker to get her into the stores. In one of them, she asked to buy a plastic bag. Partly because it felt so nice to walk around with that label on the bag. But most of it was needed to the tablet. It still was uncomfortable tucked in his pants. What she would then do with it, she did not know. There must be a later question in my apartment, she thought. If you can call that room for an apartment ...?!

Someone floor higher up she saw some telescopes at a shop. Or telescope as the common man most say. She reacted to them, to Zhinsun always talked about and wished for one. Asked why a vendor if prices. Decided to buy one and send it to him. But not today. For now she was most there to watch. Just see and enjoy everything that was put there in the store. This is the life, she thought almost constant smile. Here I want to stay.

Yin had already visited a considerable number of shops in the huge China Plaza. Out of sheer exhaustion and hunger, she could no longer walk past McDonalds, but settled down there for a hamburger. Had probably read about the restaurant chain in any newspaper, and probably thought it corresponded to her unspecified expectations. Was most surprised at how efficiently and smoothly everything seemed to float behind the counter. No dead moments where not. Counted his money in the wallet again and thought he had the situation under control ... so far. However, what troubled her, was there with the suitcase at the home of Chen. Clearly aware that it must somehow be retrieved from there. While the keys to the apartment must be returned of course. Thought it a try one morning when he certainly was not home. After the hamburger and the strange milky drink with fruit taste, she looked down into the plastic bag. Not on the tablet, which also remained there, but the two white T-shirt and a gray black stylish blouse. They had just kind of ended up there. Without someone paid for them additionally.Felt actually hosted some comfort in the form of some new clothing. Who can blame me for that? Especially after everything I went through, she thought. Took them out of the bag. Twisted and turned on them. Everything to try to imagine how they would look at her. Felt satisfied and somehow also comforted. Just as easily, it was not the thing at the bottom of the bag. Namely tablet. Took it up a little stealthily and examined it as best she could. Did not know at all how it got started it. Still less what you really could do with it. Thought for a while and came upon a brilliant idea. Of course, she would go back to the cafe next to Chen's home. To see if she could find those guys who sold mobiles. At least the kind that tried to sell her. Maybe he wanted to buy the plate. Or so he knew someone who might be interested ...!?

It was exactly then, when she was the first person stepped into the subway car, as she saw it. After first had to wait for everyone while trying to squeeze through the newly opened door. Namely a folded stack of bills lying on one of the chairs. It had probably slipped out of someone disembarking passengers' pocket. Since no one else even had time to see it, she threw herself down on the chair. Sat on the notes and pretend that nothing happened.When most sat and carriage return rolled away, she tried to sneak unnoticed into the hand under the tail. For as invisible as possible to coax the money. Nobody noticed anything either. Not even when she stuffed the wad in the bag. All the way home she wondered, how many yuan it really could be. Decided to wait to count them. At least until she was at home in your room. Once at the station, she tripped in at a local supermarket to also buy some food.

Comfortably reclined in bed she lay and counted the money. Twice a precaution. Both times she came up to 370 million yuan. Most of småsedlar. Smiled a little to himself and thought that now might justice is finally beginning to take its toll. This is probably just a compensation for the misery suffered by me, she said. Totally ok too! And she was not compensated ... she thought actually implement it yourself. For example with the shirts that are now lying there in front of her on the bed. With the price tags still there. Just as a couple of cans of fish also posted on the free account. They were still in the pockets of the shirt. Of course not listed on the receipt for the other goods from the grocery store. Without any moral qualms. Saw it instead mostly as a replacement for a former life lost. And now also as a compensation for the continued hitting of misery. A compensation according to her yet were not even near any kind of fair-leveling. Far from it.

The next morning she woke up slightly more hopeful. After a quick breakfast, she took her bag with the tablet, and set out toward his uncle's home. Now in its new stylish gråmönstrade blouse. Missing namely the wonderful perfume and the rest of the things that were left there. Had already started looking pretty good in the local area. Knew now was the shops and eateries there. Went with a lighter step than yesterday. Peered curiously into the shop windows along the entire way. Felt good cheer. Especially when she saw her new blouse reflecting in the windows. Stopped a few blocks later at the end of a side street. Namely right at the corner of the house no. 119 to Kengkou Rd. Wanted to ensure that neither the Cheng or the old lady in the ground floor appeared. Everything seemed to be quietly and safely out. Convincing enough to venture upon a try. To sneak into the apartment.First, ensure that no voices were heard inside the door. So it was with a trembling hand that the key was in the lock. Knob and opened the door cautiously. It was all quiet inside. The somewhat trapped air gossiped also, that no one was home. No longer any trace of beer cans lying there the last time. Rushed into his old room. Saw that the bed was still unmade. Could also note some blood stains on the sheet. Otherwise everything was as before.The bag was still standing and perfume too. Raking up her things and clothes and threw them in the bag. Took an extra lap around the room. Just because nothing that belonged to her would be left. With a smile, she noted a bloody fork on the floor ...!? Provided himself then with a couple of beers from the refrigerator. Before the door was locked and the keys was put into the mail slot. Now there again ... no turning back, she thought.Thoughtful and actually slightly taken of the situation.

Today's second subject was trying to find the guy with the cell phone or his friends. Therefore, she slipped back into the cafe next door. Did not see them but asked a man at the bar if they are often used to be there. However, he was not sure who she meant. Suspected that there could possibly be gang of mostly lived in the arcade game over down the street. Yin thanked for the information and went there. The sun had broken through the clouds and the air felt for once relatively healthy. At least not yet had time to mix with the exhaust gases. The odor from the intense and noisy traffic. The street was already full of cars, scooters, motorcycles, and not least ... bicycles. They gave thankfully not emit any exhaust fumes. Silence too. Longed indeed after his own bike. Whoever was stuck at home in the bus station.

After a few minutes she was there. The arcade was up-stairs in a rather run-down house. Just sign at the entrance showed that there was no activity at all. Once inside the room was far from quiet. At least sonically. Pinball Games pounded rhythmically and the music flowed profusely. The young clientele who sat riveted at the screens seemed to thrive in any case. Intensely focused as they were on their shooting and flickering games. Yin also noticed that guy from the first day at the diner. Stood slightly provocative close to him. Eventually he glanced up at her. Looked be back again and gave up a surprise ...

- But ... it's you !? The girl with the bag ...
- Yes exactly, I'm there, she replied, trying to see a little bit cool.
- And that big bag you have with you today too ... ha ha ha ...? I'm sorry, but I have not left the phone anymore. It is unfortunately sold. But ... I have a few others that are equally sharp. Can fix them up in ten minutes. It's quiet.
- I will not have any phone today, either. Just wondering if you know someone who is interested in this kind?
- Maxat! A toad from Apple. What do you want for it then? Or do you want another one, he said, grinning and stroking his hand through his long greasy hair. Does not have any in stock right now, but ...
- Do you know anyone who wants to buy it?

- If I know someone ?! Absolutely. For the right price only ...!? Join in at the office over there.

After getting the green light over the intercom door opened. There was even smokier. Yet one could see through the fog two men who sat with his legs up on the desk. The one with also a glass in hand. They looked somewhat astonished, when they saw the seemingly little alienated Yin. Rural girl with her old brown bag in his hand.

- Who is that?
- This bride has a toad for sale. Last model and almost in new condition.
- Let me see. Bring it. Does it work?
- I think ...
- Ha, ha ... Do not know how to put it on. The bride here do not know how to put on! Then we'll see ...

The man took a sip and put the glass down. Pressed a button and waited. After a few seconds the screen lit up. Yin breathed a sigh of relief, but tried to keep a straight face. He tried it for a while and everything looked more pleased.

- What were you thinking of this then?
- 370!

- 370 ...! Without charger ?! Well, you little baby. Think admittedly not that you come across it in any legal manner. And ... not that I might bother me either. But, you see, we always take a risk with this kind of thing. Sooo ... if I say 300 remain. Then you've got a reasonable price sweetheart.
- Then 350 !?
- You were a tough lady. But you, I should not be impossible. 325 and a handshake ...!? Do we agree?
- Well, 325 is well ok for me. In cash since then.
- Cash is ... yes! Can not imagine that you would like to have it in kind ... ha ha ha ...

On the way down the stairs she stopped and counted the money. Again. Most to convince himself that it was true. Slightly perplexed about the continuation of the day she decided that serving. Where the man with the dog sitting. She went there along the streets which is now bathed in the warm sun. At this time, it was also a lot of people in motion. One had to tick their way along the sidewalks. People did not seem to be stressed despite the heat. But were simply too many in number for pavement width. How right she was almost there. But neither the man nor the dog appeared at the table outside. Yin also took a turn through the room to look after him. But without result. Even so, she sat down at a table next to the window. Ordered in green tea and some kind of large almond macaroon. Sweet tooth had begun to make itself felt. For the most part came first in the afternoons.But what does it matter, she thought. Now that I still have so much money.

Looked a bit pensive as she sat in solitude at the table. Enjoyed the delicious cake while she was studying street life that passed the revue where outside in the heat. Some also carried umbrellas to get some shade during the walk. Suddenly she came to think of his workmates from the factory. Yes, his former words. The cute little Da-Xia who always smiled at everybody. Lien, was the one who learned the Yin the first time. Kind and considerate. Fang-hua was a bit more reserved and shy. But worked enough fastest of all. Her own best friend was still Min. Came from the same district as Yin. Therefore, they had so much to talk about. And that guy on the deletion. He possibly could was in love with her ...? Do not even know what his name is, did it suddenly appear for her. Was just wondering what everyone is doing at this moment at the factory and what they're talking about. Maybe they discuss why I did not come back ?! Actually, she wanted to tell them but was ashamed too much. Could not talk about it. It was too painful, all that has happened. Did not want to experience it again. Most of all, ignore it. Despite awareness of the outstanding salary that should be left to pick up. If it was not already confiscated to say. Did not really matter. Had already got tired

of the monotonous job. There was nothing that she
wanted to spend her youth days. No, now she had other
plans. Only today had yielded 695 yuan. In itself, with a
little luck ... yet.

An hour later, she was sitting in the subway on the way
in to Shang Xia Jiu. Or Beijing Road as the most known
as. Actually her first visit to Guangzhou's largest and
most elegant shopping street. Admittedly, most just to
watch and scout a little. Once among all strolling and
shoping people she ended up in a small crowd. It was
the Hero Square around a portrait painter. The artist
had probably halfway point in his painting of a young
beautiful woman. Stiffly seated on a stool right in front
of him. Maybe you have to look like her, to dare sit
there, she thought. The lady on the podium also appeared happy with the attention. But of course, are accustomed to always be in the center, so it takes it well
completely obvious, guessed Yin. There she stood behind the front row among the curious. The audience
followed the work and looked intently at the painting
itself. What the artist did and how similar it would
be. That is all ... except the Yin. She had instead had
spotted a wallet sticking out of a back pocket. On a
seemingly well-dressed man with the suit. The jacket
had namely slipped up when he leaned forward to see
better. She pretended to do the same. Leaned forward
towards the man, while the wallet slowly left back pock-

et and disappeared into Yin's plastic bag. Unnoticed she disappeared from the crowd. Without any interest to await the finished painting. Just smiled with satisfaction to himself and continued calmly on the square.

Inside the KFC she had just finished their meal with chicken and fried potatoes. One of Chen's beer cans were also empty and abandoned on the tray. Felt already a little half full. The noise in the room was her only as a murmur in the background. Thought for a while that she had lost sensation in his lips, too. But all the symptoms disappeared immediately, when the purse was taken out of the bag. Also sang a bit for himself while the contents were spread out on the table. The three payment cards and papers were in a pile. Other papers and receipts in another. Then the fun started. To figure out the notes. They were not so many, but the higher denominations. Hardly dared to trust their limited math skills, but the total ended up on her unimaginable ... 2200 yuan. Noticeably trembling hand when the money was transferred to the wallet. Without any scruples emphatic that unnecessarily burdened her conscience. It looked like I said just as a way to compensate. For the misguided fate unconditionally hit her. Debit cards did she still not, how to use. So they broke apart and fell into the basket from leftover food. Along with receipts and other papers. Thought for a moment if there was no use for Papers. But soon realized that it could instead bind her to the theft. So it was also broken in two. Although I am from the country, but stupid is not I, she thought, and spread out the pieces from coffee mugs and drumstick in the waste bag.

After flanerat a while along the street past all the enticing shops, she decided to purchase a pair of pants. Light blue jeans had long been on her wish list, and now it was time. They not only had jeans in the store, but all kinds of clothes. The difficulty was that literally sticking to each shelf and rod with gorgeous garments. However, came eventually to denim department. Mark patches of different sizes were as pure jungle for her. Was finally forced to ask for help. A friendly but very made up girl guided her to a pair that actually fit perfectly. Yin twisted and turned itself. Looked in the mirror and could not help but smile a little. They sit as cast and is also suitable for the blouse, she thought. It's my day today. Felt next obnoxious then forced to take on those old pants again. It is all too easy to get accustomed to luxury and beauty, she realized. With the receipt of the hand left the checkout. Excited and also a little proud. Now with even one of those stylish shopping bag in hand.

It was not long before the shoe shops also received visits. In one of the shops she found a pair of white sneakers with red stripe along the sole. And with laces in the same bright color. They were maybe a bit too expensive, but what did it matter. Easy come, easy go ... Easy come, easy go ... as they said in American films. Felt also found that the new money probably was the conclusion. How and from where did she not, of course. But intuition signaled the certainty to the brain in any way. Self confident that prophecy she let wallet bleed out another couple of times. During the voyage of discovery through the impressions vibrant shopping street. You simply could not resist. It was like a New Year's celebration in the square.

Mentally and physically exhausted, she was forced to retreat. With hands full of designer bags, she went reluctantly back towards the subway. A small RC car suddenly wandered about among the legs of her. The pilot of the craft was a sailor dressed boy in short pants and hat sitting on a park bench next. The rest of the sofa was occupied by his elegant smoking mother and her shopping bags. A lady of class with short black skirt and shoes in the same color. Furthermore, with diamond sparkling earrings and dark red spectacles during the hair up. She read a book and did not seem to care. At least as long as his son did not disturb her. But instead only devoted himself to the car. Yin came immediately to mind his brother. Without any similarity in general. He would like to have one of those car, she thought with sadness. Maybe you should buy one of those instead of the telescope, it hit her. More fun and more useful probably !? When the boy had run three laps around her, she became noticeably irritated him. Took Kit with one leg and kicked the car with his foot. It flew a few meters away and ended up upside down just in front of a cyclist. During the wheel of a stressed and inattentive cyclists woman who unfortunately did not have time to swerve. Yin heard fastidiously everything clearly but looked the other way.Continued as if nothing had happened. Heard However, the boy's screams and his immediate appeal to the mother ... "Mom, she was ..!? That ugly old woman. " Yin noted the comment and also their upset argumentative with bicycle woman. The two quarreling women heard all the way down into the underground decline. But Yin could not listen more. They have certainly afford to buy a new car, she thought his defense. That brat feel safe just fine by little setbacks in life. Have probably already gone long enough that famous shrimp sandwich. Every day spoiled served its always so chic one-child-mother. Yin sigh of any kind of resignation and lead. Thought of the Chinese proverb ... "Without clouds, we would not appreciate the sun" .... Half stumbling down the stairs, she managed just an oncoming train. Self surprised that she actually was homesick. Home to what in any case was a place where one could retire for a while. Cook some food. Pull a blanket over his head and just sleep out. Charge the batteries for the next day. Think about what the next day's fate could offer. Which way the future of her hitherto random adventures would take. She did not know. But curiosity would be the last that left her.

Woke up quickly the next morning. A restless dream helped her disorientation. Did not understand why a completely unfamiliar light in the ceiling so uncomfortable staring back at her. Had not noticed it before. Usually, just press the power button in the evening and then carefully made their way to the bed in the dark. Lifted uneasily on his head but could not immediately exhale. Got namely see their shopping bags standing lined up against the wall in the room. Suddenly remembered everything. Turned around in bed and snuggled back down under the blanket. Pleased snuff on a little longer.

That's right ... she thought. When she was awake an hour later eagerly jumped out of bed. Alternating with dressing even started the breakfast to be fixed up. Was strangely eager to go back to the town again. Had namely got a brilliant idea. Did she herself anyway. Picked out the jeans out of the plastic bag and put back the receipt. After a half-hour she was going. Now with one of his new t-shirt wearing. A light blue with any Western text.Without caring about the meaning of words, it was with pride as she sat there in the subway. Could barely stop himself and his eagerness, when the escalator too slowly took her up to the Beijing Street. A few blocks away, she slowed up the ladder. Crept slowly up to the entrance and walk the store's elegant glass doors. Carefully peered in to see who among the staff who were there today. Did not recognize them from yesterday and slid therefore quietly into the room. Walked around and looked at the goods. Just like a regular customer. The drug, however, more and more toward the denim department. Had carefully memorized byxstorleken the patch back home and found pretty soon an equivalent pair of shelves. Looked anxiously around, as she stood with her jeans in her hand. Another customer picked and were also among the trousers only a few meters away from her.Moreover, everything seemed to be ok. Without anyone noticing, slid his pants down in the bag. While she slowly pulled away towards the cashier and the exit. Watched carefully cashier moment was busy with another customer. At the next appropriate occasion she increased the speed. Quickly went and stood behind the customer at checkout. Pretended as if she had just come in from the street. Stood unmoved and calm and just waited for their turn. The client was a middle-aged woman who paid their goods by card. Yin studied the procedure with the card payment carefully. Might be useful to know some future time, she thought, and got ready on his case at checkout.

She greeted kindly at the cashier. Took up the jeans and the receipt from the bag and placed them on the counter. Explained that the pants maybe felt a little too tight and that she would like to do a buyback. In accordance with the conditions of sale which was printed at the bottom of the receipt. As she firmly put it. The girl at the cash register looked surveyed her. All the while she studied receipt. Then examined the jeans carefully. Quite obviously, in order to convince themselves that they really were in original condition. The rest of the case was a matter of routine. First, just type in a different receipt and then sign for their 169 yuan. How hard can it be?Not at all, she thought, and walked out of the store with an empty bag in his hand. Instead, with a further addition to its own cash. Still with jeans at home in the apartment. She smiled triumphantly. Then strolled for a change along the cross streets. Just to window shop and watch the world go by. This balmy and beautiful morning in Guangzhou. She was in good spirits. For the moment, without any thoughts of his immediate past. After a while she slipped into a pastry shop. Or rather a cafe was well. Almost as if it has become a new habit for her, ordered her back into the coffee. Habit and habit anyway. It was actually only the second or third time in their life. A steaming mug of the black beverage was on the table. Together with a large addition cream cake. Now it's just a cigarette missing. Thus, to look like one of those true lady, she thought dreamily. But already after the first bite of the divine good cake, she corrected herself. To start smoking, she would certainly not do. Besides, it cost money. And the use of them had a completely different priority right now.

All the while the pastry disappeared from the plate, amused herself by studying people who passed by. It was then, while she sat by the window and enjoyed life as a brand new idea began to take shape in her head. It was so tempting that she is already on the way from the cafe began to realize it. Searched long for a business that sold bags and finally found a shop with a large assortment. After careful consideration, she decided a kind sports bag with zipper on top. A relatively high, oblong and spacious thing in dark blue color. Moreover, with a stylish mark on the page. Not that it had no bearing on her idea, yet. A little more class on everything that was bought here and now in Guangzhou, began to actually become like a new hallmark for her. Yin from the country. Though really just a matter of course. Fully in line with her long ago unfulfilled dreams. Was already so excited about the idea that even the necessary cutter was purchased by return. Although only a small detail in this context. But still a necessity for the plan would be executed.

Had just settled down on a wooden bench in the shade of some tall bushes. In a small almost deserted park found by chance. There she went immediately to work. Took out the bag and scissors. Carefully cut inside and along the perforated edge of the bottom. Until the entire bottom plate fell out of one piece. Threw it into the bushes and put the rest of the bag on the couch. It was actually completely alone ... after all. Superficially looked more or less like before the surgery. Admittedly it was not the same statute in it, but it had no meaning. At least not for that it would be used. Hypo also pulling the handles on the double zipper. Tried function and felt satisfied. Then took the bag and left the park. Upholstered first available taxi and ordered it away towards the eastern railway station. The same station that she not long since arrived.

Paid and got out of the taxi. Saw the big clock above the entrance was at 11:50. This day begins well, she thought expectantly. The high murmur and speakers echoing reminded her of when she came to Guangzhou. Even the sight of all travelers jostling with each other. This is of course the perfect place for the mission, she said to herself. While she calmly and methodically strolled around the premises. However, still with örnblicken connected.Gazing constantly looking for suitable items. But the minutes turned into an hour and felt increasingly doubtful. Would this delicate task really succeed? Dared not really decide the right moment. Nor was it's totally risk free.Which she understood very well. Even so, it was something that attracted and excited her. Probably it was both risks and opportunities. Probably also the feeling of actually dare. Himself took the risk but also the entire profit. Skruplerna was she who said long ago put on the shelf. This was not for the squeamish. It had to have the mental strength. And she had.

Later on one side of the arrival hall she saw an exchange. Where people stood and queued. Looked like just ankomna travelers with bags of all kinds. What most caught her gaze, however, was an elegantly dressed man in a suit and shiny black shoes. He was not the sex, but stood alone leaning against a pillar. Talked all the time engaged on his mobile phone. Gesturing sometimes with the other arm and seemed even slightly upset. Just behind him the closest pillar stood his briefcase in brown leather. It certainly had been standing right next to him from the beginning. But during the conversation probably unwittingly strayed a few meters away from it. Yin understood immediately that his time had come. There was no time to lose, and without hesitation she went to work. The protection of the pillar, she approached the portfolio. Looked around before, to check if anyone else noticed her. When this was not so, she put quickly their sports bag over leather bag. Upholstered hand down through the preset gap in the zipper and grabbed the portfolio handle. In the few seconds it was all over. With the portfolio inside the fabric bag strode calmly from there. No one in the room could not see anything other than a little girl with sports bag slowly and nonchalantly walked out of the station. What then happened to the man, did not bother her at all. Quickly became a closed chapter in her brain. Instead totally focused on their catch. In the relatively easily caught fish. It is now just waiting to be gutted. But it will have to wait until I'm home in the apartment again, she thought, and found their way to the nearest underground decline.

Once aboard the way home she thought of how the bag could be opened. Peered down into the gap and saw a gold combination lock four digits wide. Realizing that the code itself would never figure out. Instead, more a question of how much violence was required. Of course, had no tools at home and decided to buy a screwdriver. To begin with, anyway. Thought that the situation there in the wagon felt somewhat comical. Here she sat with a bag without bottom. With another bag inside. Also on the floor. Toyed with the idea of get up and go away. With just a sports bag in his hand and briefcase standing still. Wondered how many people would respond and if so how. Perhaps they would be so surprised that no one was able to say anything? No, probably would be their first thought may be that there were two cases that originally stood next to each other. And then certainly some kind soul to her attention on "the forgotten bag". That is, if the carriage was relatively full of people. Otherwise earliest thrown across the portfolio, as soon as she left the carriage and the doors closed. They were, after all, in China, for God's sake. But on the other hand, should she not herself have done the same thing. There was no denying with. It was already proven, if you say so.

With a local Purchased screwdriver she sat once at home on the edge of the bed and pondered. With the portfolio just next door. Decided first to satisfy his hunger. Before the massacre began. Cooked up some noodle soup on the gas stove and served it with bread, sundried tomatoes and salami. She loved the sausage. Moreover, it remained well without a refrigerator. Looked thinking between bites off against leather portfolio. Felt almost like the hunter who had just closed down their prey. And then sit by the fire and lubricates their gizzards. Felt a bit like a feast in all its simplicity. Although she did not even know if it actually contained something of value.Could of course be a BLANK ..!? But adversity was something she was used to. Nothing that permanently stopped her to move on in life. In this case, not even essential. There will always be new opportunities and bags are plentiful, she thought. But at the same time and given the risk that the dividend should be in reasonable relation to the dividend. Which she would soon find out.

Ugly marks was the only one who appeared on the portfolio after a few minutes of breaking and prying. It was difficult to access with the screwdriver. No good and large enough gaps anywhere. Therefore, she changed tactics after a while. Fetched a pot from the galley and thought to use it as a hammer. She pounded and twisted. Swore and snorted before suddenly something gave in. It was the lock that came loose. Ended up on the floor in a few pieces. But even though it was not the fight over. The portfolio did not open at all voluntarily. Soon saw no other solution than to jump on it. Only when it was down on the floor, she saw the hinges at the bottom.Began digging with the screwdriver in the bare metal that clung to them. Since it did not take long before "Sesame opened". Hot and sweaty after the fight with the bag, she could finally look down into the treasure chest. A variety of brochures and paper first caught her attention. Expectant she continued her examination of the content. Paper, cigarettes and other uninteresting she laid in a heap. The second in a special. When the bag was completely empty, began her pulse beat a little faster. Saw namely already interesting things in the later pile. Apart from the vial with any kind of colored whiskey similar alcohol. Namely, a travel case unfortunately only found to contain a pass and something that probably was a used flight ticket and other travel documents. The surprise she got when another exactly like the plastic cover was opened. Namely, containing a stack of foreign banknotes with a rubber band around. Studied banknotes long and carefully but did not understand the foreign text. Still, said to her that the money could probably be worth a lot. Maybe a lot even. What did she know?

With the wad posted on the table and the rest of the content returned in what is now the remnants of the once fine leather handbag, she sat heavily down on the chair and admired the glory. For some reason she remembered suddenly that one of the two beer cans from Chen's floor still remained in the apartment. It comes as a gift from heaven at this moment, she realized. This must be celebrated. Poured out of cans in an unwashed glass. It was certainly not cold enough and foaming significantly. But it was such that one could endure. Especially when this kind of relatively risky assignment gives so good dividends. That is the minimum reward one can indulge in the midst of solitude, she said. Drinking slowly and really enjoyed the bubbles in the mouth. Almost started to like this drink, too. Just as with the coffee. It previously not attracted her very much. What can be worth, she thought of between gulp area. Dared not even guess. With the risk to only be disappointed when the truth would eventually come to light. Felt more and more lush in the head. As the contents of the can reduced. This must be a strong variety, she thought. Without putting their own little frail body in relation to the amount of alcohol in beer. A relatively healthy reaction of such a young and spirits inexperienced woman. An established fact that she actually had to settle. There does not any more beers in room safe. The light intoxication still got her dreams to wake up. All the clothes that might be purchased. To cut out and get a new hairstyle. Sitting on the restaurant and be waited on. Nice shoes. Jewelry and perfumes. Then she suddenly remembered her perfume in your suitcase. Took up the little bottle and sprinkled a few drops everywhere. It was celebration for God's sake!It smells divine, she thought. So good, that maybe is not any point in wasting money on other varieties, she thought. No, she was satisfied as they say in poker circles. And a certain type of gambler she actually. For no ordinary moral and squeamish girl of her age would have achieved what is now honored her. So, if you left the moral bit behind, she was actually worth it.

Stolen happiness

The following day found her in front of the entrance to one of the offices of Guangdong Development Bank. Stood outside and stepped a little unsettled. Wanted one last time to repeat his statement where she got the money.If now the bank would wonder, to say ?! Had only brought half of the banknotes. Namely ten. Most of that amount was not suspiciously large. But also because she could more easily work out the banknotes value together.Had the honor of the day taken on a new sweater, his new shoes and moreover neat combed through the otherwise volatile tousled hair. A costume dressed elderly man in glasses took care of her case. He flipped through the notes. Examined them also against a lamp. While he occasionally cast an inquiring glance at Yin, which she quoted lightly shaken. Just as if she were some kind of prostitute who now wanted to switch the weekend worthwhile. He reckoned, however, quickly through the money. Typed on the keyboard and waited a few seconds. A paper was printed. Then counted the new banknotes in the door. 1000 US dollars will be ... 6 121.48 Chinese yuan, said the cashier and shot over exchange receipt and the money to Yin. With some coins top of the top. However, she was too busy with the whole situation, to take in how much she really had. Stuffed carelessly into the wad in his little wallet and removed quickly from the bank premises. How much is it, she repeated to herself? What could it be? Could not wait another second, but sat down on the stone steps right outside. Took out the bundle back and read through the receipt. 6121 ....!? Was it possible? Six thousand one hundred twenty-one yuan! Well, apparently it was so. Counted through them again and everything seemed Meeting. This was then extended its cash with a further six thousand pix !? Then it should therefore be equally at home in your suitcase ... according to the simple mathematics. A lucky star must have been lit over my head, she thought. Maybe it's my turn now ..? Can it really be so?

Dreamy strolled to herself along the street for a while. Until she once saw that the café. Where the older man with the little dog used to hang. Yes, used and used ...? Last time he was not there. Went though the street and found him rather than inside themselves serving this time. The dog became quite wild when it discovered her. Constantly tried to jump up on Yin therefore sat down on his knees. The tail was like a windshield wiper in the pouring rain, and her face was just as cleaned. Apparently it came remembered her from the previous meeting. Which is also the man pointed. It was namely seldom so where excited and happy otherwise. Yin acted up a while with Yang, however, calmed down eventually. The man asked, what most of all liked to eat. Thought namely, to invite it to a little tidbit now that her cash was so well stocked for once. It ate apparently anything but raw fish, he claimed. So Yin asked the staff to cut out a suitably large piece of ham as it could get gorging on. The dog was almost as happy again when she came back. Especially when it got grit on the actual pork bitten in the hand. Then it was no longer focused on Yin. But only on the buttocks as the willing chewed itself. Asked the man if he could buy her a cup of tea with some snacks. The man quickly put down the paper and bent gratefully repeatedly. Almost to Yin felt a little embarrassed. How strange it was still not. Yin also ordered a coffee for himself and a few donuts without holes for both of them. They sat for a long while and talked about everything. It was found that he had been captain once. Told me about some of his travels around the world and Yin listened with curiosity and wide-eyed. Even asked him about how people looked and how they lived in other countries. Sucked interested in themselves of everything she heard. Fascinated by what you actually could do and where in the world they could travel. If you only had the money. Yes, for us that is not ship captains, ie. They may of course all that stuff in the bargain. Imagine, if one day life will experience only a part of all that, she thought. For while he told me about his life and his experiences, was Yin and her thoughts are already far off in the distance somewhere. Almost like having the ability to teleport there. He wondered, of course, who she really was and what she did in Guangzhou? But Yin, like a clam, slid deliberately a little of the truth. Told instead a somewhat sanitized story about himself and his life in Guangzhou. Did not want to expose themselves and their origin for other relatively unknown people just like that. For truth has no value yet in this situation, she thought. Not for anyone else anyway. It is probably difficult for myself.

But after one hour's conversation with each other across the table, she did not bother him anymore. Without thanked for himself and hugged dearly if the dog one last time. The man bowed deeply with his head and hands in the usual greeting gesture. Laughed and said goodbye to her. On the way back, however, the thoughts most dog. Long awaited after the. Imagine, if you still had your own of those dog. What fun we would have, she thought, somewhat melancholy. For deep down she knew that it was just a dream. In all cases, the moment of life. There were too many other things she wanted to do first. Then it struck her suddenly. The name of the dog, she knew, but not sjökaptenens. It felt a little awkward. But on the other hand, had not he even asked for her. So, for me, he may remain captain, she decided. It was still the dog which she loved.

On the way home she stopped at a newsstand. Bought a few magazines and some candy. Fashion magazines with many pictures, of course. With them thought she was to spend the rest of the day at home in bed. Just cuddle and dream away from the fine clothes and stylish people. To the world that now just waiting for her. A world that smelled so good. Where everything was marvelous and beautiful. An existence where misery and sorrow did not exist. A happier life simply. In addition to amuse themselves with newspapers and chocolate, she would even plan for tomorrow. The day when the time for the great change had come.

The rain sprinkled down through the windless smog-filled air. It was not cold, but an unpleasant smell of wet cobblestones disgusted her slightly. Also became remorseful because she already gained an umbrella. Even so grateful to not become too wet when she småspringande finally came down into the subway. For further transport to China Plaza. She knew what awaited her there. The plan for the day was already fixed. Now things would change in her life. Not dramatic indeed ... but still. The salon was selected previously. An elegant studio on level 4. A place where everything seemed to be of the highest class. A reputable salon with a stylish interior and staff in uniform modern clothes. Yes, almost like uniforms could say. It at least gave a professional impression at first glance. Had now decided to cut off his long hair. Wanted a short elegant and more easily maintained pageboy. A variant, which she had seen in fashion magazines. Had even cut out a picture of the famous movie star Zhang Ziyi. On the picture in a page with bangs. Apparently called hairstyle China Bob ...!? How or how.She showed in all cases the clipboard for the female hairdresser and explained to her how she wanted to have it. Should just be nice to get rid of this long and flygiga forelock, she thought.

About an hour later found the mirror a different person. Is it really me, she thought, fascinated. Was more than happy and could not help but feel the miracle. Let your fingers pleasurable glide through the black surge. Was most fascinated by the fringe. It really changed her charisma. Now for a more cool and mannequin-like look. It was the new Yin simply! Expensive it was! But it's worth it, she said. Felt somehow more feminine too.Already in the escalator down, she saw her own reflection in one of the display windows. Almost resembled a mannequin. It must be the best grade you can get, she convinced herself. Now, this was only the first step in her metamorphosis. The next stop in the luxurious Plaza China became a clothing store. A deal with garments almost in the Chanel style. Fairly strict in color and cut but elegant and of very high quality sewing. With the idea that "only the best is good enough," she glided into the shop. Even here with a cutout of a kind outfit with a jacket. Also, a movie star, of course. The clerk showed a very serious interest in her tastes and desires and led her farther into the store. After many visits to the test cab led increasingly to a final choice. It was a gray jumpsuit with waisted blazer in a thin woolen material. The jacket is also lined with purple-colored silk. The gray tygknapparna had rose-colored edges as well as the edges of the jacket kind. The clerk showed her even a discreetly patterned white blouse with a round collar. For a cerisfärgad scarf with black stripes. The icing on the cake. Yin reckoned together the prices for all the garments. Thought for a while but could not resist the temptation. Despite the 2390 yuan as the party would cost her, she hit. Despite the surprisingly unconcerned about the amount. It will probably secure more money eventually, she thought as she counted out the notes at checkout. Also had their stylish brand bag and left the store both proud and elated. What if Mom had been part of this. Just got a glimpse of her in the stings. And brother then ...!? That's right! Suddenly she remembered. The radio-controlled car! Did, however, exactly where she had seen such a store before. Brought the big bag and went there. The range in there was huge. Here was everything. At least when it came to toys, hobby items and gadgets in general. Also, aircraft, helicopters, and something called Quadcopter were on the shelves. A sort of flying craft with four propellers. How now worked? Looked rather than right on the cars. Where was the availability and variety is also great. Soon found a car in the appropriate size. One that she thought looked both colorful and cool off. Including radio control of course. Even got some batteries for free. Probably because she had chosen a more expensive variant, she thought. Or so it was, that she on the way to the checkout just found one of those small radio set. Just the kind she imagined. A red version with black round speakers. Finally, the room would be filled with human voices and beautiful music. So, even a large bag in her arms, she went on. Be especially happy for Zhinsuns sake. She remembered the car. Would first just home and make a package of the box. Then send it back to the village. Would he be happy, or ...?!

Before she left the store for the day was the visit to the shoe icing on the cake: a. A pair of black low-heeled patent leather shoes with red soles. They set a cast and she felt blessed in them. At the same time convinced that they fitted perfectly to the jumpsuit. And the scarf too. With several bags in hands, tired feet and light tension headaches, she could just not go past the cafe down there on the next plane. Felt mentally stunned when she sat down heavily in one of the upholstered wicker chairs. You can be tired even to shop, she realized while the waitress took up her order. A coffee with milk and a pastry ... again. You have to enjoy while you can. It had now become her motto. Next time, she thought, when I've jumpsuit and all the rest of me, I'll sit here with coffee and cake. The freshly painted red nails world accustomed blazing on a cool cigarette. To get to know how it feels.Just for once, that is. Before she left China Plaza this time, purchased the course that red nail polish. Even a pink lipstick ended up in the bag. After it felt the day virtually flawless.

After a light meal at home in the room she fell asleep. Lying on his back in bed with an open newspaper on his chest as usual. Woke up much later, and then noticed that it is already dark outside the window. Ooohh ... if you still had a radio, she thought disappointed. Longed namely for some company. In the radio belonged to at least people who talked and moreover beautiful music. When the newly awakened brain get enough fresh oxygen, she was clear head and remembered the radio. The one she had just bought in town. Completely ripped out of the box. Joined to the network. Pulled up the antenna and found a station with typical Chinese music. It became Music FM 99.3. Melancholic and beautiful tones filled the room. As a change of pace against loneliness and the silence that constantly tormented her. The music and the thoughts of his solitary position in the big city suddenly got his eyes watering. Tears began to doubt to roll down his cheek. The handkerchief was soon a wet ball and got replaced. A couple of times additionally. Out on the town felt a loneliness is not so obvious. There were so many other things that distracted. Surrounded by people on the move as they always were. Now in the evening forced emptiness she tried also to console themselves with a refreshing cup of green tea after the day's labors. Suddenly remembered that liquor bottle that still remained in the leather portfolio. What could there be in that? Took anyway it. Opened the screw cap and pulled spirits vapors through the nose. It smells anyway good, she thought. Sipped gently on the drink and grinned bad. Not the taste without the strength of the same. Burned admittedly in the mouth but otherwise it was probably nothing wrong with it. On the contrary! Pretty cute actually. Tried therefore to mix down the booze in the half-full cup of tea. Filled up to the width. Understood of course that there were liquor of any sort. But did not care so much. In the cities have the other habits, she thought, and took a large swig of the now diluted lukewarm tea.

The evening passed with reading newspapers, radio, music and even more cups of tea. All additionally mixed with half alcohol. Did fact that it was an excellent combination pure in taste. The spirits are not burned flavor and sweetness processed in any way. It was even tastier and tastier. One must probably just get used to, she reasoned. The music from the radio made her also to sing along to the songs. Admittedly rather than good. But at the same time made it her in a better mood. Laughed sometimes at some hilarious thought that went through my brain. Thought smile and foresight of all bags that may soon be whisked away in the sports bag. It feels so funny, she thought. So surprisingly easy and simple to what one might think. Thinking even on the more sites that could operate on. Therefore went away and picked the fabric bag. Put it on the bed and just laughed. Devils in the sea! Consider that I have come to this. Now felt almost compelled to re-open the suitcase and take up the bill stack that still remained there. In order to ascertain that it was true. Then threw up the notes in the air and let them fall like snowflakes over the bed. Turned up the volume on the radio. Laughed and sang. Among other things, a song that her mother often gnolat at home. The laughter was mixed, however, soon with tears and even more handkerchiefs went for. At the bottom of the suitcase, she dug then presented a rolled up sweater. A whose content was found to be a plastic bag with anything inside. Sat on the bed and unfolded the bag. Took out a shiny black pistol and looked worrying disrespectful to it. Even though it was loaded. Where did you old man's bastard, 'she said aloud. Though now most slurring. Ubbdjäävel ...! Ha! Here it is! Do you get that !? Your gun. It can look for until you die ... asshole. Ha, ha ... you pig. Threaten my mother with this ..? No you, now is the end of it. Forever. This should I throw in the river. Do you understand it ... huh ?! There you can of course look for it, she cried scornfully to the fictitious image of the stepfather. Tried thereby violating the epitome of him. At the same time, she roared with laughter at the absurd idea. Namely, that he also could not defend themselves. But almost as quickly as galghumorn taken command of her mood shifted again. Again became serious and his eyes darkened. Took a firm hold of the gun with both hands. Stood up on wobbly legs and aimed towards the window. Actually, we should shoot it where the creature. He jumped on me in bed. That fan at the home of Chen, she said menacingly. Aiming straight arm while the gun precariously swayed to and fro. Talking to himself, to concretise their ideas and their stifled hatred. If he were here now, I'd pull the trigger right away. Absolutely! My forehead too. Bang ... Boom ... goodbye! After another half minute threateningly aiming towards his invisible considering figure, she lowered the weapon. Then dropped himself more or less together on top of the bed. Slurred any last words before she silencing completely. Sleeping in a sort of fetal position.

The morning after she woke up lying on its side with faint music in the background. Alerted to something that tickled his nose. Without opening her eyes she felt by hand. Just seemed to be a paper that she tried to wave away. Instead became aware of his crackling dry mouth, which apparently no saliva was left. Was terribly thirsty and unfortunately even some nausea. Opened his eyes so that she could see that paper. Which, however, proved to be a note. One of the stack of the six million yuan during the evening like streamers frisky floated around the room. When she saw the gun down at his knees, began a blurred picture of last night is slowly becoming clear. Certainly yes, she thought, and sighed deeply. The damn booze. Then lift your head and slowly sit up did not feel as frisky. It was just another proof that alcohol can really do the trick to bring headaches to life. The lesson was immediately enrolled in her throbbing head. This I will never do, she thought dejectedly. Matthew sitting at the edge of the bed with nausea strongly on the rise. Immediately shut off the radio. For every minute that went, she felt that the inevitable was coming. Soon it would happen, but how and where ...?! Looked desperately around but saw mostly just walls floors and ceilings. Yes, plastic bags of course. But rather, she would vomit in bed or on the floor than in any of them. There she was in any case quite clear about. Suddenly she realized that it was time. Hourglass last grains had just fallen heavily down through the hole. Timely as a gift from God, she just views on the pan. The rest, as they say ... just history. Certainly not by the appetizing variety, but nonetheless an inevitable consequence of the so-called sinful lifestyle.

The subsequent miserable morning is not something one normally writes down in her journal. Rather something that quickly relegated to the concept meaningless days disappeared. And so did this ... eventually. Remarkably, however, that even after the day not filled with any content of value. The problem was also strengthened by that Yin had not that much food at home. Just drink water and chew on some dry pieces of bread did not just rehabilitation easier. The gun was deported back to bundle in your suitcase. Like the banknotes, which also found the back there. During the same rubber band plastic case where they had been before. So everything back to square one. Besides booze bottle of course. It was now just as vacuous as the "day after" can often be felt. However, after the weak bones still made it out and purchased some food and drink, began forces soon return. Thoughts of the future sprouted once inside. Actually looked forward again. Devoted even a moment to package the radio controlled car. Intended to send the next day. After a refreshing long shower in the corridor, shower room, she spent at least a couple of hours to try their new clothes. Unfortunately, without a mirror. Got instead try to see himself in the painting reflective glass. Despite the transparent picture of her new look she felt reborn.So incredibly comfortable and natural in that elegant wardrobe. It was like ... she ... simply. Could hardly wait for the day after. To the day when she decided to make his entrance as Lady Yin. She jokingly called himself. At least when epitome of her new revelation was the boldest. Also this day she fell asleep, before it was to a close. Dreamily to great music on the lowest volume.

Freshly showered and precariously splashed with her eau de perfume she went down the street toward the subway. In the cross-cool jumpsuit, in his pageboy and the contrasting black shoes. Had first planned to take a taxi because of the hazy and humid weather. But realized that more people should get to enjoy her stylish mirage. Which they could get if she went collectively. Did may not itself behavior but her hidden exhibitionist side began increasingly to appear. Pressed now up to the surface. To obtain more nutrients from the surrounding sphere of desire and admiration. Even some younger men turned already on her. When she was a first-class concubine glided through the crowd. Felt somewhat moth Place in the worn and overcrowded carriages in the metro. Will not at all to my right in this environment, she thought. Got off at the station Shang Xia Jiu Street in Beijing, and continued her catwalk up in the ground. Looked expectantly at the men she met. Namely whether and how they would react to her revelation. Therefore became more and more confident when her expectations also came true. Saw namely the corner of my eye that they were watching her. This is different than at home in Gouzishan, she thought. There, do not turn anyone if by anyone at all. A paradoxical thought as she now most hated men.At least some of them. Of quite obvious soul besides. However, tried for a moment to forget all that. For now it was more important things going on. Mastered steps towards a nearby post office. Would be to send the package to the radio controlled car. Home to his dear brother probably longed as much for her as she did him. Though probably even more. For what he had to look forward to at home. It was not that much. And so very many playmates, he had not either. Surely he longed for her. I'm sure he thought she was on the way out. Despite all satisfied with the package now at least it was on the way. Had also enclosed the old lady's delicate necklace with a small greeting to the mother. It's the least she's worth, she said. With the addition of the handwritten patch that more would come. When that day came. She was still her mother and what had she really been without her ...?!

Had not eaten anything that morning and slipped therefore into the first best restaurant. Yes, that is ... not just the first. Without that met the requirement of a certain exclusivity. Namely Jinhao Chaoshan. Well there ordered a groovy tefrukost. With everything on ... you could say. Sat at a round mirror shiny black table by the window. With a red carpet beneath. Really sucked into the classic atmosphere. Further into the restaurant sat an elderly man and played nice relaxing music. Namely the one in which the horse head fiddle. Yin was already familiar with that type of violin. For her Mongolian grandfather had had a similar one. Even if it is not used as often. Had most worked as an ornamental. It has a square body and a neck with just two strings in between. The neck at the top also looks like a horse head. Yin ate with great appetite and soon felt the spirits wake up again. Her metabolism demanded much food at specific times. Which she often neglected. Studied world go out on the sidewalk from its excellent position closest to the window. From where they could not see her through the dark-tinted windows. Knowing that made her a bit more comfortable. Mostly because she felt less observed. Nice to be able to sit there and undisturbed get check out all that passed revue outside. For example ... What is she wearing, anyway? Why is he so strange? Are they really so dear as they look? Ooohh, what color of hair. How can one allow himself to haunt themselves out like that? Go and drink coffee ... oh well ... hurry maybe ..!?What a sweet lady. She can carry all that stuff all by yourself !? In the age addition. But, the ugly tattoos he has ... everywhere. Imagine, when I get that stuff white hair. May not live long enough ... who knows ...!? Ooohh, such a cute little girl. Festive! The same color of clothes as her mother. I wonder if I will ever have any children ...? Gladly one of those cute little kid. No, now I feel full. And a little drowsy, actually. Much food there was.Sitting enough for a while and take a look. Is so fun anyway. Really interesting and inspiring indeed. So went the tanks back and forth.

Fifteen minutes later saw her strolling down the street. Now yourself as observed by the other. Maybe even by someone in secret behind a window. What did she know? Felt still calm and satisfied. Curious what the day would offer. Felt is a need for a toilet. That rooibos the tea seems to be diuretic, she noted, and looked around. Was looking for a suitable place. Continued a bit further. Until she passed a hotel. Namely Jiahong Hotel. A very stylish place with a man in uniform outside the entrance. Suited therefore to seek the toilet there. A little more class on sanitation will not hurt, she thought, and walked confidently toward the revolving door. Screen The hat made a welcoming salute, and soon she was inside the stunning foyer. On the shiny stone floor was a lot of people in motion. Many about as elegantly dressed as she once was. Both men and women actually. Felt immediately comfortable in the surroundings. May perhaps even be my new paw chips, she realized happily. Impressed by the futuristic interior. The high ceiling and all the spotlights on each floor. To which circular elevators constantly went up and down through the transparent glass tube. Moreover, sofas, tables and carpets, no second-rate goods directly. Rather, the "state of the art". Strolled around a bit timid in the foyer and looked.Finally found the door of the women's symbol on.

It was probably some sort of conference at the hotel. To view an adjacent room heard an intense murmur of voices. Yin peeked in and saw a huge smorgasbord groaning. It seemed that the party was in its final phase, for some of the guests were apparently on their way from there. For a moment she thought brazenly just walk in and help themselves to the goodies. But changed his mind as quickly. Still could not get down a bit after its steady breakfast. Instead went out to the open foyer and sat in one of the luxurious sofas. Was there substantial aware that she was one of those who have not owned a handbag. For all the other women seemed to have provided themselves with. The small detail she had completely missed. Grieved a little because of it, but instead took the opportunity to bask in the glory together with the exclusive clientele. Tried to see as urbane as possible. Added with one leg over the other and took up a glossy magazine from the table. Did not even notice myself that she was holding it upside down, the thoughts and the gaze was somewhere else. What a place, she thought! To also have the privilege of living here, was something that went high above her imagination. Certainly not cheap either, she assumed.

After resting for a while and melt all the new impressions, she went to the front desk just inside the entrance. There were some ladies and conversed. Just behind them stood a rack of postcards, which she absent-mindedly looked through. Nice pictures, it was but a few short thought she still did not send. Not yet awhile. There, she had decided. Studied however, the postcards for a while and then turned on. Looked dreamily out over the mighty palace courtyard. Really impressive, she thought. Fascinated that you could build houses in that way. However it was, it caught her eye on one of the young boys hotels. He, too, in style according to a uniform. He looked back with a puzzled look. Hesitated at first, but approached her then with firm steps. Bowed apologetically and asked ... about the lady perhaps wanted help with the bag out to the taxi. Yin viewed surprised down at a low red abandoned suitcases. Whoever she is only now became aware. In a few seconds passed a thousand thoughts through your head. But during the first few seconds to understand what he really meant. Then began the gray cells to process the paradoxical information. The bag ... taxi ... the lady ...!? My bag ... my ..? Out to the taxi ...!? She looked alternately at the bag and out onto the street. Looked into his eager eyes and looked back toward the bag again. Then heard herself suddenly say ...

- "Yeah, I ... thought ... take a taxi ... to the train station.
Then saw it all then played out spirit in a film. Saw the bellhop take a firm hold of the bag. Saw himself trotting after him through the revolving door. While the man in uniform made an elegant salute and wished her welcome back. A door into a taxis back seat had opened. Without being able to fight back, she found out soon sitting there. Heard trunk slam. Simultaneously with the hotel boy's oral instructions to the driver. Namely, to drive her to the eastern railway station. Tried to answer his short dutiful greeting outside the window but could not move his arm. Sat almost as paralyzed when the taxi is beyond her control slowly rolled away from the hotel.

On the way to the station, she would obviously have to change your destination. But all for mentally busy trying to sort out what had actually happened. And why she has not been able to to cancel the whole thing. Did not understand that it really was her subconscious that gave her the green light. That is ... to do nothing. Let everything happen and just follow without protest. Somewhat contradictory convinced herself however, that as long as she did not take the initiative, so she was innocent. It was not she who asked for help with the suitcase. Nor proposed a taxi and certainly not one who stopped into the bag in the back. In addition, closed the door and ordered the car to the station. No, she was simply a victim of the situation, surprising and rapid processes. Although she constantly deep down knew that it was not on a par with ordinary human morality. However, if there was anything dangerous or her disadvantage, she had understood it all stopped. However, it had she not done. Every other man should at least known by his bad conscience afterward. But Yin's empathic abilities as usual was never as great as her intelligent cunning. However, she felt instinctively from afar, when it smelled money. And this suitcase really stank of just that.

Fortunately, she had enough cash to pay the taxi at the station. The suitcase was equipped with wheels also became an easy match for Yin. All the way home on the subway went like clockwork. Looked at times amazed and smiling down on the surreal red the thing that she dragged around. Could this really be true! Such are lucky to have one just does not, she thought. Without really knowing what lurked inside the bag. At worst, it could of course just consist of a lot of men's clothing and nothing else. But on the other hand, I at least got a nice new suitcase, she reasoned. Now if you could open it to say. Without significant damage additionally !? Which as proven was not the case with the former. Namely leather portfolio.

Once home, where outside the house, she met the janitor. Or whatever you'd call him. He greeted and asked, Yin returned home from a trip. Denied, however, his friendly request. Considered that the journey from the hotel via the train station and the hit could not be attributed to the epithet ... trip. Found instead that she bought a new bag. He swallowed the lie with the comment that it would be good to have. Asked her too if everything was ok in the apartment in general. Yin complained, however, that the water in the showers sometimes not warm. All too often icy indeed. Got at least the hint not to shower after blackouts. The water cools namely quickly, he asserted. Desired her since a good day. Problems like they probably did not hear about, she thought, and went into the stairwell.

The bag was relatively heavy, she felt the stairs on the way up. Something is there anyway in it, she thought hopefully. Once inside the room immediately began the inspection. However, took the first off the elegant jacket and kicked off his shoes to the other side of the room. Was both impatient and curious. Felt really hungry, but the matter had caused. Food is in this moment a very low priority, she said. Had already in the subway disappointed found that even this bag was labeled with a code lock. Four wheels with numbers. Switched on the radio for some exhilarating music. It may be good for the brain, she thought. Then sat on the bed with the bag in front of him. Thought for a moment and then began to try different combinations. For example ... One Two Three Four. Since the same numbers in reverse but without result. Tried also with a variety of other combinations. Unfortunately, with the same disappointing outcome. Took rather a reluctant pause to instead make to order some food. Later, as she sat there and ate in her loneliness, she saw the broken leather portfolio on the floor farther away. Became even more convinced that the red suitcase was actually too nice to be destroyed.

Resumed eventually their almost hopeless attempt by the code lock. Had for a while yet tried the combination of four identical numbers in a row. Began with four ones and tested it. Continued with the idea and when she came to four sixes, felt something in the lock. The last sixth grade went namely so easy to set up. While the bag steel edges were moving slightly. A gap arose and Yin were clearly to himself. The bag was open! Absolutely unbelievable !! Hoped she understood. But never that it would really go. Four sixes! The owner was a female sex, she had almost figured out because of the red color. But now it became even the contents confirmation of it.Some colorful panties, bras and make-up stuff was lying on top. Her first primitive thought was ridiculous enough only if the panties could possibly be in her size. Further down below some fancy shirts, blouses and tunics lay a black fur jacket. Wow, she thought. I wonder if it is true !? It seemed indeed as smooth and comfortable, but the thought still not there. Also noticed that something heavy was wrapped in it. It proved to be a folding machine. Type laptop that she had seen in many of the stores at the China Plaza. It sees both new and expensive out, she thought. Although she was not at all familiar with the industry. Well, not really with computers at all.There was nothing that they could afford in the country. Maybe not direct any use for them either, she said. At least, her mother and stepfather always said that.

Discovery journey in the bag went on to more interesting things were discovered. Namely, a pair of shoes, a charger, a tourist map of Guangzhou, deodorant and perfume bottle. The last two were in a carrying case along with toothbrush and similar things. However, there was also a box in elegant black leather that immediately aroused her interest. It had a lid with gold text on top. When she expectant and cautiously peered at it, revealed some jewelry. Among other things, a refined gold necklace with a large uncolored cut stone that sparkled wonderfully there in the lamplight. Also another similar with a black faceted rectangular stones. In a pendant that dangled over the gold chain. Yin was overwhelmed and felt almost euphoric when she took off and got to know the treasures. Because they really were genuine, she was completely convinced. Although her experience was not particularly great in this area either. It was in any case absolutely no novelty. As such rubbish you could buy in the market stalls at home in the village. Hardly! She then also found a pair of stylish shoes and a few items of clothing no longer felt so interesting. Was now mostly fixed on laptop computer, fur jacket and jewelery. They constituted themselves the treasure in the treasure chest. That the shoes were too big, she looked directly. Did not even try them. The suit, however tested one by one, and many of them sat surprisingly good. Almost as if I bought them myself, she thought. The rest of the day passed also in try CONDUCT OF THE characters. The garments went on and off. And again in different combinations. Matching with different necklaces and bracelets. The earrings she had unfortunately no benefit yet. Not until the holes in the ears were made. It had never even been on the table for her at home on the farm. It is such where the nonsense that you are doing in the city, had her mother always told her.

Middle of the night she woke up to some kind of inner voice. Dazed, she came in, it must be next week I fill 17. Half asleep half awake. Reassured, and assured of the truth she fell asleep straight away. However, it was also the first conscious thought struck her the morning after. Must complete 17 years, she thought, and kicked off the blanket. 17 years ...!? It was not so long ago we celebrated thirteen, she thought. And now ... no one to celebrate with !? Low therefore easily distressed for a long time and thought about his fate. Although partly self-chosen yet, she thought. Felt deserted and melancholy, until the idea came up. Of course! So it must be. Of course, I will invite the girls from the factory that night, she thought, and jumped out of bed. Now, when I can afford it and everything. What excited them to be !? Came while she must also communicate to them the truth.What had happened and why she never came back to the factory again. It was difficult, but it did sting quite easily. First, she must just find out exactly what day it was. Date had never felt important to her, and even less in Guangzhou. Here you can live only in the present moment and not elsewhere. The bank must she. Switch out the rest of the banknotes in the stack. It should be celebrated, so be it. That was after her motto.

Once inside the bank branch, she even find out the current date. Ie Friday and then realized that the birthday was already on Tuesday. For safety's sake, she had chosen a different bank this time. Yes, banking and banking. It was probably the most foreign currency exchange. But even here someone wondered, where she got the money. Got an almost equally large sum yuan this time. The course had been altered slightly, but what did it matter.Felt still richer than ever. And then she had not yet sold a single little thing from the suitcase. Which neither seemed particularly urgent. Have so I can do anyway, she thought. And throughout the weekend, there was also plenty of time for planning av17 anniversary with his old comrades. The first thing that struck her was that they could celebrate the birthday of the cafe Chawan. Besides, it was a nice place, so she was fairly familiar with the staff now too. The sailor and the dog may also be involved on a corner, she thought. If they happen to be there, that is.

<u>Chawan</u>

The weekend ran quickly past. Yin took the opportunity for some sightseeing around the town. One day, she was, among other things down the Pearl River and strolled around. Enjoyed the walk under the beautiful willows along the beach. Felt however, somewhat lonely as usual. But met by chance an elderly couple who played the accordion and sang there. They were so intimate and dashing in any way. Were themselves quite easily. Threw a coin in their outsourced hat and even stopped for a while to listen. Was any reason eventually even a little familiar with them. It turned out that they were Mrs. Li and Mr Yau. Pensioners who took the opportunity to make a killing, while delighting the surrounding area with some entertainment. Not at all wrong, thought Yin afterwards sat for a long while and talked with them. Was also invited for a cup of tea and a slice of the cake that Mrs. Li himself baked. It was so nice and cool in the shade of the willow. On wooden sofa where they sat and drank coffee. The chirping of small birds bounced curiously around them. Looked praying up. Just waiting to be any dropped crumbs from the cake would be within reach. Now and then passed the occasional boat or barge out on the river. Sometimes muffled honking. It all felt like a fine art photography. With höghusens grådisiga and blurred silhouette in the background. A fantastic beautiful view. Soothing waves from the boats rolled simultaneously toward the riverbank. Lapping against the stone wall and then bounce out again against the next wave.Under the influence of this hypnotic ambient suddenly an idea up. Now if you still are having a party, so why not top it with live music, she thought. And what would be better then than Mrs. Li and Mr Yau ?! It soon turned out that both knew the street where the cafe Chawan low. They also had both the desire and time for an hour gig that evening. 300 yuan, thought she was a fair price additionally. They confirmed the agreement with a handshake and a hope for a nice evening together on Tuesday evening. Yin stood eventually and thanked him for everything. Reluctantly left the nice couple and resumed their ride along the promenade. However, soon heard from a distance how their music again began to sound. From park benches farther behind. There at the Pearl River beautiful beach.

After an interesting visit in the old city Xiyin in Liwandistriktet became then a few rides in the roller coaster at the Amusement Park. Also enjoyed the large candy supply where in the park. While she took the opportunity, to amuse themselves royally with the various attractions that were offered. Of course it was also a little shopping as a perfect finale on Sunday evening. People Life on Beijing Lu is namely the most intense in the evenings.Especially during weekends. Then the pedestrian street was full of young and old of all varieties. You can really see how they seem to enjoy it public street life and the atmosphere there. Feel enough in some way as part of something big. As citizens of the world perhaps? A social and commercial intercourse which was not at all obvious to just a few decades ago in China. The younger of course has not the historical perspective with them, but can probably feel the uppblommande freedom nonetheless, one can assume. Although Yin, or especially she might, felt the future and destiny targeted gift. Grateful to be part of everything and to be a part of the city's vibrant life. For her mother, for example, this was by no means a foregone conclusion. More a kind of glittering life that was far away ... somewhere. Yin often thought about her. More and more as time went on. The so quickly ran through the hourglass down in Guangzhou. One can not directly say that she was homesick. But sometimes she missed her advice and support in their autonomous but scant loneliness. Therefore, she took on Sunday evening courage to visit the girls in a factory pavilion. The spartan place where they grudgingly lived. All jumped down from the beds and utterly bounced around with joy when she suddenly and unexpectedly made the admission in their cramped and simple lair. All admired the new short hairstyle. Fingered admiring, curious and a little envious of her new clothes. The questions rained down on her. Where had she been? Why? What did she do now? And so on ... and so on. Yin sat on the floor like a chief at the campfire with all the girls in a semicircle around him. Told and explained everything to the best of ability. Hugs succeeded each other and tears fell when she revealed everything about the rape. Felt that she had to put all the cards on the table. Yes, almost all, anyway ...!? Although she had hitherto done most to repress the unpleasant, it could still be nice to finally cry out with their friends. They have now remained. All felt really with her and also expressed his hatred towards someone who could do something so disgusting. However, most were still most happy that she was back.Except possibly one of them. It was the shy Feng-Hua. She already after a moment thought she had had enough. Pulled instead demonstratively up to his överslaf with a book. Anticipated in any way that all that could hardly be true. Especially for the answer on the origin of the Yin received all their money. Namely that the benefits of horse games. I thought she was just not on. Not even when Yin stated that Chen himself also played had taught her all about betting on horses. The other girls swallowed, however, mostly without questioning her significantly. They were most fascinated by her stories. Also understood really why she wanted to come back to the factory again. Now that she apparently earned so good at those horses. They themselves would not have come back, they felt. One of the girls got up and trimmed a few cups of green tea. Then continued the conversation until late into the evening. Although several of them already yawned wide. In view of the girls' job early the next day, she went right from there. They were all now informed. If what applied and where they would go on Tuesday night. Luckily, it was not so much overtime work in the factory at the moment. Apparently had something with the world economy to do, they had heard. Once back home in the apartment she struck immediately on the radio to relax with some music. Found a change a quiet moment adequate supply of Radio Guangdong at 103.6. Mentally relatively exhausted but also overjoyed, she crawled to bed this evening. Felt actually not so lonely anymore. One conclusion that she just had time to pull before the tanks eventually imperceptibly floated into the subtle dream world.

Monday passed with various preparations and cares for tomorrow's small party at Chawan. First, she visited the cafe and ordered everything that could be served. For safety's sake kept even the staff of musical entertainment that was orderly. They were only positive for her initiative. The other guests could of course then also get a bout of the ladle. As thanks for Yin's commitment promised the head of Chawan to invite all her guests at the ice cream. It is only to thank and receive, she replied happily. The couple with the accordion, however, would come first at eight o'clock in the evening, it was said. Then the guests at least got themselves some food. The dessert makes itself perhaps better to singing and music, she thought. And hoped that the girls would agree. They were hardly spoiled with entertainment. Either at work or at home in the dormitories. There was not much time to enliven the soul. It was most trying to rest a few hours. To be able to get up in time, and then the hurricane to get through the long days with all the hard work. There was really nothing filmstjärneliv which they lived. It had Yin thoroughly learned. Only during the short time she has been there and slaved. Felt rather privileged and knew at the same time, she was there. Actually had a bad conscience, and therefore wanted to do as much as possible for these four girls. She had firmly set itself. Although it would cost her some money. But what, a little more jingle in the coffers to be fixed quite easily now, she said. It is only to act as a lock and key beginning to appear. However, it was still a way to go down there. And absolutely no danger to the life of the party executive. On the contrary! Even after the monthly rent for the apartment, there were plenty of bullets left. She had come here to live his life. Not to worry about things that might not even occur. On the way home she bought with her no adequate party gadgets. It was colorful balloons, streamers, badges and other eye-catching novelty. What she thought would be at a party.

Tuesday did not start well. Namely headaches. In addition to their egen17 birthday. But it is usually easy, just coming up, she thought. Segade however out of bed to cook some breakfast. The pain subsided, however gradually. Slowly, but as the breakfast gave her new energy. However later in the day, she began to feel a slight nausea. She never otherwise used to suffer from it. In addition, on the occasions when too much green tea mixed with half liquor, ie. But then you get really blame himself, she realized philosophizing about it. And although the discomfort from stomach subsided in the afternoon, luckily. The rest of the time she was fully occupied with, to get ready for the evening. What to take on, she thought, looking among their own and the other so-called "acquired" clothing. Almost all the jewelry was only part of the latter category. That is stolen or originated by the agency of chance. Regardless, she felt proud and beautiful there in front of the mirror. The sparkling and shiny objects tested one by one. And then she had not yet assumed any matching stylish clothing, but just stood there unglamorous in panties and T-shirt. Which, however, required a good imagination. Namely being able to conceive combinations without having to get dressed. Which she still considered doing. Decisions The anxiety was palpable. Not that it was so remarkable about a small party on any insignificant brawn in this district. But still. Wanted to be in his favor now that she for once in their life, they had the opportunities.Strangely right too. She was, after all, only 16 ... or yes, 17 years and a girl from the country.

Already afar you could see the color palette. Café Cha-wan lit up the dark street with her for the day colored lamps, colored balloons and part-streamers. No passerby could err on, the place was equipped for any type of party that evening. So was the fact, and the same thought even the girls from the factory, when they smile made her entrance at the cafe just seven. Yin was of course already there and welcomed them with both bows and hugs.While they utterly astonished at her own revelation. As a true lady in Hollywood, she stood there in front of them. For the day of a newly purchased qi pao. A dazzling beautiful indigo-colored long dress with high neck. In a shimmering fabric that glittered so charmingly in rislampornas light. Over the shoulders of the relatively thin black fur jacket. Elegantly matched to the black lacquer shoes. The necklace around his neck was not of this world. Dyrgripen, as derived from the case of the red suitcase. Barely understood how much it could be worth. And certainly did no one else does either. Besides Fang-hua ... maybe. Looked namely suspiciously at the fabulous necklace. She was the most pragmatic and critical thinking of the girls. Saw more objective and careful consideration of everything in his environment. So even on Yin's outfit this festive evening. If that's the diamonds that shimmers so beautiful, they must be worth a fortune ...!? There she said through loud to her friends. Before the whole gang laughing and revived continued into the festive dinner table. With red lanterns on a white cloth. Deep inside the café's cozy corner. Everyone wanted to know the dress and jewelery. No one dared to ask, however, what it all had cost. Somewhere they understood of course, that she must have come in some unlikely way to make money. Especially considering how she looked and was dressed in the factory. Moreover, not so very long ago. They were as fascinated as they were confused about her. If it was so easy to win on the horses, why was working when so many remain in the factories? The thought certainly more of them during the evening. But no one said anything, of course. Everything was so festive and fun. And for once, they could forget their otherwise so stringy and backbreaking life. Therefore, they also took the opportunity to enjoy the food and all the others who were invited. Yin got a picture of them as gifts. It was Da Xia who had painted it. She was namely the gang with artistic gift. It represented a Chinese joint-fisherman standing in his boat in the evening. With a pair of cormorants birds on board and a brilliant lantern hanging in the stern. In the background the dark silhouette of the high mountains. She said that it represented her father. Who apparently was also joint fishermen. Yin thanked everyone for the board. Bent and showed their sincere appreciation hands together in front of him. Especially against Da Xia whose skills she admired.

The first was served to the red wine, was the so-called "long-life noodles". A common right on birthdays. Soup bowls of noodles and poached egg which then a good sauce poured over it. All yarn is then chopped ham and green onions. Most Chinese people feel very familiar with the law. Usually a safe bet that also this was to their liking. After that, he commanded the head of Chawan on the good ice cream, he had previously promised. All talking at each other, while they took the refreshing delicacy. Had a good time in general. Everyday life felt even far away. For they had much to vent. Even long after the meal. Told many hilarious stories from the factory.Something that also Yin found interesting. Chawans boss had on Yin's order even made a cake with 17 candles. A creation that eventually carried into the Society's applause. They had just started with the cake, when two elderly people unexpectedly popped up from nowhere. A woman and a man with the accordion. Both of some kind of national costumes in beautiful colors. When they suddenly broke into song and games, watched the girls just surprised at each other. However, soon realized that the whole thing probably was part of the celebration of Yin's birthday. Though completely unaware of Yin's previous meeting and agreed with Mrs.

Li and Mr Yau down at the Pearl River beach. Something that she did not even later told them. It can get to be a little secret, she felt. All considered, however, that the whole thing was hilarious and entertaining. Though some stray guests further away in the restaurant clapped too fond. After timing seemed all be satisfied. And so even Yin understood. Although impressed by the older couple's large and varied repertoire. Something that not even she knew of in advance. Also from them, she received afterwards congratulations. Ms. Li also praised the elegant dress and it pleased her. They felt right then almost like her mom and dad, she thought. But the fun ends. So too this party.However, not until a few hours after the wife Li and Mr Yau left Chawan, so bent and thanked all four girls separately. Satiated, happy and satisfied, they went home in the late evening. Yin was however left for a while to help with cleaning up a bit. Some of the debris had actually she pulled there.

Mr Chuanli, which took Chawan, then asked Yin to get into his little office behind the kitchen.
- Well, Yin. First I have to thank you for choosing us to celebrate your birthday at. It is always nice with new guests and also good for us as a company, of course.
- Yes, but it felt like the right place in any way. And so is it's relatively close too.

- Yes, it is understood. Aahh ... yes, I was going to ask
you another thing Yin. You've met Mr. Bohai this before. He was with the little dog. I know right?
- Oh, you mean the sailor? Yes, I call him that. Did not
really his real name, actually. Yes, I have met both him
and the dog.
- This is how Yin, that's Bohai Sea, yes sailor therefore
does indeed have had a stroke and is in the hospital
now.
- No, what are you saying ?! What a shame!
- Yes, it happened actually right here at the cafe for a
couple of days ago. We found him on the floor next to
his table. He was conscious, but spoke slurred and his
eyes were only directed in one direction. We immediately understood the gravity and summoned paramedics
course.
- I understand really. So sad, as I said. How is he now?
- My wife Li Juan has visited him and it is well like
that. No further actually. He is paralyzed on one side,
and apparently can not talk. But he gets all the help that
can be given in all cases. I was not here when it happened. But the staff took care of his dog, and right now
is the home of my wife. Otherwise we will bring it to
here. It is so wise and cute. Sat faithfully beside Mr Bohai and licked his face, when the staff found
them.Lacking enough his master course. Located namely, sometimes on the floor over there at his regular table,

and whimpers. How much or little it understands, knows, of course not.

- Then I have to come here and visit one day, when it's here. I Love Yang!

- Yes, just like you said. Yang called it. And ... it was actually what I wanted to discuss with you. Because we work so much, both my wife and I, so we wondered if ... you ... possibly ... could think of to take care of it until further notice. All here have seen how good you will agree. The dog and you thus. I know right?

Yin stopped a while. Also saw a little worried. My thoughts went round in his head, and she understood clearly, what in that case would mean to her freedom to come. Had already thought about that dog before. Even after the first time they met. For a dog, she had always wanted.

- I could take him to the test for a while. Yes, just to see if I can handle it, quite easily.

- Sure! It was also as we had imagined it all. If you have not had a dog before, there may well be a little strange at first. You can not just think of himself anymore. So it is understood.

- No, that was exactly what I was thinking. They want to see if it works with the rest of their lives too. Otherwise, I love dogs. Absolutely no doubt about it.

While she said that, she remembered the feeling of loneliness that often hit her at home in the rental room recently. This spartan room with four bare walls could not
get anyone to suffer from dark thoughts. And amidst all
this so I offered now a dog, it dawned on her. Maybe
even your own dog. If now is not the sailor feel better
about themselves that is.

- Ok! I'll try it for a while then. Only I get some tips and
some help with dog food and such. Have no experience
at all of that. Perhaps you can understand?
- Of course! We will send the dog food that we
have. Then you can anytime come over here and get
some leftovers. Things that often gets over in a restaurant. Tomorrow my wife Li Juan also work here, and
then he can take with Yang hit. If it suits you, you can
download it then? Or?
- Yeah, otherwise I will have to take the time, simply. Wow, what a thrill it will be!

It was with light steps and a few hundred yuan poorer
as Yin later went home in the dark. Full of expectation,
yet anxiously pondering. It will be a big adjustment for
me, she thought. But she always used to say. You can
not worry about the future all the time. But may bring
problems if and when they may arise. With the certainty
inside she fell asleep safely that night. Seventeen years

and nearly a day old. Now also with a Mergansers fishermen standing beside him on the bed table.

A long-awaited friend

Yin's reunion with Yang day after was a tumultuous history. The dog howled with delight when she appeared on Chawan just after lunch. The dog little tail wagged like never before. Jumped incessantly against her and calmed down not until Yin sat down at the floor. And allowed it to lick her face. Only then was the time to greet Mrs. Li Juan. She laughed at Yang's joy and noted with satisfaction that some more well-liked math would probably be difficult to find. And was not needed either, what she knew of Yin's loving hugs. Eventually they took Yang with him into the kitchen. There was already a bag of dog food, dog treats and other appropriate accessories for a prospective dog owners. Among other things, a couple of different lines of which Li Juan mount one of the dog's collar. Pointed out while Yin, the dog had just eaten and drunk. Would get by for a while.Also sent a matschema guidance. Something Yin already yesterday demanded. This was too new for her and all the advice was welcome. Self she also received some food from the restaurant back home. Li Juan had filled a paper bag with a club sandwich and a soda. For both she and Mr Chuanli was so thankful. Yes, to Yin wanted to take care of the dog. At least to the test.

Their first walk through the neighborhoods went splendidly. Although drug dog eagerly on the leash, but it was nothing compared to her overall happiness. Found it hard to take in the whole experience. Realizing, however, that she finally got her own dog. Hopefully! Another one of her dreams fulfilled. She was totally concentrated on keeping the dog on the right course between the people they met. Not curiously sniffing each person. And it went fairly well for a while. Just had to show who was boss. Which was also the Council to her by Li Juan. Long ago, she felt so proud and happy. Maybe it was the loneliness now a thing of the past? It was all the same, what she hoped for. At home in your room, we can play and cuddle with each other. What fun it will be, she thought, expectant, as they walked along the sidewalk this warm and beautiful day. It would not, however, remain the quiet walk which was first conceived. For after a short walk got Yin instinctive. Namely, that someone went too close behind her. By chance she glanced while obliquely into a skylfönster. Saw, besides himself, also a man just behind him. With arm extended toward the back. How much could she perceive the mirror image of the window. But Yin reacted with lightning speed! Cross Riveted both himself and the dog. Turned in fractions of a second. Behold, a middle-aged man with two sticks in his hand. One of which during the actual turnaround hooked into her jacket pocket. The man was apparently shocked by her sudden and rapid cross turnaround. For when he would turn around and flee, he stumbled on his own feet and fell headlong to the ground. Yin got hold of the stick, just when it fell from his pocket. Found themselves quickly and took a few steps toward him.Defenseless and surprised he lay still on the ground. Put one foot on the chest and forced him to stay on his back. Shine struck with the stick toward the face to scare him. The second swab was lying on the ground next. Yin understood immediately that it was a pickpocket caught in the act. Who, if not her, knew how such things could go to. Admittedly method with two chopsticks as extended fingers, a new variant for her. It all happened in seconds and the person who responded almost as fast Yang. Ran barking toward the terrified thief and even did a fake. Most of the pure instinct of course, but also of fear and to protect the Yin. It did not have to think. It was just a question. Just as the nature was programmed. Some people stayed up curiously, wondering understood, what was going on. The sight of a young girl with foot on a prone man and an excited barking dog next door. It is clear that such creates attention. While others totally uninterested just went on. They seemed to be accustomed to the strange occurrences around town. Also wanted to not interfere. Especially in events not touched them. Yin shouted a few choice phrases against the man, when he tried to break free. All the while the dog continued to highlight their dissatisfaction with him. Barked like that fiery that only small dogs can do. Hesitated and did not know what she would do with him. Noticed However, soon he was difficult to hold on the back. Therefore closed the whole with a well-aimed kick in the ass. With a shrill cry he quickly got back on its feet. Ran confused from there and disappeared into the crowd. Like a thief ... on the day.

Even some among the audience, who did not really understand what it was all about, applauded anyway. Probably thought it was funny, when something different was happening in the otherwise dreary rhythm. After calming the dog down she took the opportunity to pick up the other stick. Pocketed both. With the ulterior motive that they might be good to have ... sometime. Then took a firm grip on the leash and continued his abruptly interrupted virgin walk that new dog owners. Exhaled and continued with confident steps from the crime scene with the locomotive Yang ahead. Clearly relieved by the unexpected event output. Understood of course that she could not have any moral views on this were the thief's actions. Especially not considering its own history which actively operates in the same industry. Defended yet his reaction that he got what he deserved. Longer than a kick in the butt, she would still not have gone. Mainly considering how reluctant she wanted the police involved. Could even be called self !? What did she know? In the worst case, recorded by a surveillance camera.No, this had to not arouse too much attention with his presence. With the wisdom sounding in her mind, she continued promenade. With Yang at the head eagerly sniffing nose. Eventually came to a small green. This fits well, she thought. For this, I can unleash the dog and in addition play around with it for a while. While getting applications for balls and Frisbees in Yang's accessory pouch. There was also a color colored dog vest with pockets and zipper on top. It did however remain there. Once released on the lawn ran the dog overjoyed around in circles here and there. When the balls came flying through the air was a joy complete. It felt like the waiting for those balls all the time. Perceived that immediately come back with the ball. Drop it in front of Yin and excited waiting for the next draft. When the Frisbee as a change thrown out over the lawn, the dog showed samples of real artistry. Caught it elegantly into the air almost every time. Sure, it had trained on this earlier, she realized. The type of acrobatics and timing was absolutely no obvious or congenital. In addition to Yin estimated whimsical and fun game, she tried to work out a little obedience while. Additional advice from Li Juan as she thought realize gradually. But why not start right away, she thought, and tried with some elementary her exercises. It showed already there, that it could lie down on command and even wait in place. Bit unnecessary, it felt almost but of course only an advantage. Gave it strategically some candy now and then. When did as she wished. Only during the more than one hour they were there and acted up, showed the sample so much skill, that further progress would only be felt as bonus. But she would learn it all. So it was thought. They would be friends for life, she understood this. There was no doubt. Unless sjömanen the unlikely recovery. Which all obviously hoping for. Although Yin ... after all.

She appreciated the silence and the beautiful surroundings of the park. Green scents broke through the smog and exhaust fumes in a refreshing way. No one is spoiled in Guangzhou. It was a sunny and relatively clear blue day. The tree branches swaying easily in the weak wind. A green oasis where the district all the chirping of small birds seemed to have gathered. What are the hyper-ventilating Yang curiously followed his gaze. But only with the eyes. Tired and eliminated as it was lying on his stomach in the grass. While Yin took the opportunity, to provide himself with the soda and club sandwich as Li Juan so prescient sent with. Really grateful for her thoughtfulness. The dog however, was too tired to beg for food. Would later rather get some dog treats to nibble on. Conceivably, when the cooling of the body reaches a more normal level. Pant with his tongue out made it impossible increasingly eating for a while. Yin however, provided himself with delights with gusto. And with good conscience additionally. Even a math have to eat now and then, she thought, and looked long with love down on Yang. Was not alone anymore! Felt an indescribable security hearty embrace happiness throughout her. Not alone anymore, she repeated within himself and stroked her hand sensually through the snuggly-soft fur.Almost like having maternal feelings. Meanwhile tumbled got the thief's old chopsticks out of the inner pocket. What am I going with this to really, she wondered. Probably you have to be quite dexterous to use them. And I'm certainly not, she noted crass. Threw them because the nearest paper basket next to the park sofa. Then let the heavy eyelids fall down for a while. Exhaled and let the wind rustling the trees form a kind of background choir with accompaniment by the chirping of the birds. Nice to relax and dream away for a while, she thought. To take the opportunity now that you have found the right place. A bit away from folkvimlets throng and stress.

Later, on the way home she suddenly had an idea. It was actually Yang gave her spread. As usual, she did kind of thing immediately. Looked for a while after a suitable shop selling handbags. However, those in which designer handbags without any just cheap copies. Gladly a couple of worst quality. Well, because she wants to buy two ...!? This was because, in order to disembark the plane that now more and more structure was in her imagination. Found a couple of pretty ugly for a cheap price. Actually in one of those gadget shop where everything costs twenty yuan. So just forty pix of a brown and a black handbag. Not just a few bags to carry the fur jacket, if you say so. The actual preparation of the plan had to wait until tomorrow. For it was with rather weary steps that the two are now set our course for home.

Once back in the room later in the afternoon, she let the dog in peace and quiet feel in their new territory to make themselves more at home. Turned on the radio with some soft background music. Also hoped that the dog would like it. Wanted to create a kind of home atmosphere. Picked out all the clothes and stuff out of the red suitcase. Replaced them with the extra blanket that was in the apartment. Shot into the open bag under the table, until the raised lid took the edge of the table. Had thus created a small cozy nook for Yang. A secluded place with a roof where it could withdraw if it felt like it. Roof over the lair is apparently something that appreciates dogs, she had read somewhere. When she after a while settled to rest, wanted the dog of course come up in bed. Despite the nice hut Yin built for it, got it, of course there. Crawled voluntarily next to her. Probably because it understood that she was the security personified. Eyes closed snuff and cuddled down his nose in

Yin's armpit. All the while she relaxed with a newspaper. Not only the dog felt tired. Because of yesterday's celebration, and this day as a new dog owner and everything. It can be tempting to just anyone. Even young and healthy 17-year-old country girl, she thought. Soon fell asleep both. Spacetime stayed up for a while in the small single apartment. Where they now lay next to each other in bed. So tightly together that only a math with his dog can do. For the first time in both their lives besides. What besides death ... would now be able to tell them apart?

She woke up the nyhetsuppläsarens voice. In the radio as apparently been on all night. Talked about some kind of typhoon or storm that had just reached the coasts of the Hong Kong. Once on the way up over the mainland and Guangzhou. Yin noted that the strong wind has already made itself felt outside the window. Maybe you should listen a little more often in the news, she thought. Saw the same time that Yang did not care about any approaching storm. On the contrary! Heard on the breath that the dog still slept quietly. However, had moved down toward the feet during the night. Sweaty feet is apparently an odor that dogs do not react negatively. Maybe just a neutral fragrance among all the other, one can guess. Many desired enough, that man also had that ability. At least, sometimes at specific times ...!? When Yin heard all the news bulletin and opened her eyes, she felt a dull nausea dawning within him. What is this now then, she wondered somewhat anxiously. Nausea again ...!? Just as a few days ago. Have not eaten anything inappropriate now? Pulled off his blanket and sat up in bed. Felt that the room as well as tossing in any way. Had been dizzy before, and was reminded of that feeling again. Damn it, she said loudly and irritably. Turned to the side and saw Yang's head sticking out from under the blanket.It looked wonderingly at her with his head cocked. Just switched the angle of the head ninety degrees here and there. Despite its declining prosperous status, she could not hold back his laughter. Felt actually a little better, just to see those big thinking eyes. And ears that stood straight up. Crawled out from his blanket hut to lick a bit on the hand. Perhaps the most to show that the thought of her. Or perhaps it was because of her groaning and relatively pale revelation this morning. Their first along furthermore. This day does not start well, she thought, and felt reluctant how the nausea increased. Got however view of an empty plastic bag on the floor next. To bend down and pick it up was apparently the trigger. A few seconds later pulled the diaphragm contracts and gag reflexes did what they could. The dog looked astonished at Yin who sat with his head inside the bag. While rhythmic primitive vocalizations ejected. When the nasty bit was done, she resumed exhausted its horizontal bed rest. Must swallow several times before the emetic center decided that it was enough. At least for this time. Yang stood right next to the pillow and looked down at her mercy. The whimpered a bit but then began to lick her carefully around the mouth. Thought to make her clean and nice ...!? The mildly special scent that arises after such a vomiting perceived probably just as one among all others for the dog. It had to be that person with admiration realize.

Yin slept well one hour, while the wind whistling grew in strength outside the window. Step up to a final and took a bite. But shelved now the rest of the day's plans. Get to train with Yang tomorrow instead, she realized. Maybe we can even start with some exercises at home in the apartment instead ?! For they had registered on the news, that they should stay indoors if possible. The dog may be the even blow away, she thought, and scratched it just behind the rävliknande ears. Asked then produced two cups of dog food and water. The dog was, unlike Yin, so far from nausea as you can get and ate with great appetite. Slurped also in the water, which surely half ended up outside. Even so, she could not help but smile at the primitive table manners. Laughed and thought the meal was sheer entertainment. Despite the aftermath of its own distasteful starting in the early morning. Had it not been for the dog's presence, I certainly felt worse, she noted.

The wind took so strong sometimes, the pane cracked. While rainwater skvalade as a whole rapids outside. Her decision not to give out, confirmed by all she saw and heard. Felt soon so ok, the indoor training with the dog could start a little bit. Yang realized at once that something was going on. Dogs can somehow read people's thoughts. Mainly through for us imperceptible signals that our behavior sends out. The waved expectantly at the tail. Looked up at Yin developed the newly purchased hideous handbags. First let the dog sniff them. Then put one of them furthest towards the front door. Asked herself with the dog in the other side of the room. It might be sniffing at the bag in her hand. While she pointed and urged to go and retrieve the bag at the door. Did not understand what she meant, but had to first be brought to the bag and literally get the handle blocked in the gap. Then again from square one. After a few rounds did it soon hint. After it ran away and took the bag. In each run through. Always let down your bag on the floor in front of Yin. Just as the instruction to. Always let the dog sniff the bag in your hand first, before it was ordered off on his mission report. In this way she got it, to associate the bag with just what it would fetch. Praised also with a piece of dog treats. But only during the first few times. Then the fun in the game to be a sufficient motivation, it is thought. Had namely done something similar with the ducks at the farm. Although their learning ability was not at all on par with a dog, of course.

After one hour of training they gave up and took a break. Yes there is, the dog's coffee was just some water and a handful of dog treats. Self took the yin a large cup of warm green tea and some biscuits. Along with them, and some magazines she crept up again to their accustomed position in bed. After first lighted ceiling light for a little more light. Yang had already found its place under the table in the suitcase. Yawned wide and half-closed his eyes. Restuarant apparently already in his futuristic designed red hut. And why not ...? Many dogs would probably be envious of such a snug and cozy den. Yin immersed himself in a fashion magazine, while the tea sip for sip disappeared from the cup. Leafed slowly through the photographs. Sometimes envious sigh for someone handsome creations in delicious color combinations. Could soon not resist the temptation of the images on these models in their gorgeous clothes of the latest cuts. Felt compelled to tear up some clothes from the pile from the red suitcase. For a change she tried a skirt. Something else not used very often. It was black and slightly patterned with bright horizontal streaks. Might suit coat lapel, she thought dreamily. Found a strange previously undiscovered thing. Namely, a black tie. Which also was finished tied and ready to use. Was looking forward among the clothes and found a white blouse with a collar. Ideal for dark tie. Then took on themselves the combination. Along with the black lacquer shoes. Topping it all off with the fur jacket on top. Since it already darkened outside the window, got glass pane serve as a mirror. A decent substitute for the mirror was missing. Happy with what she saw. Did they have found a style that suited her. May well get used to wear a skirt, she realized with some legitimate doubt.

Boiled up some water for even a cup of tea. Not that she must directly, but mostly to let off steam and divert the thoughts of anything else. Found at the same time an old bag of candy that once insisted on her attention.Munched down the treat one after the other. All the while the water boiled. Understood of course that it was not comfort eating, he devoted himself. For thoughts were somewhere else. Yang, who immediately heard the bag rustling, was soon below with begging eyes and looked up. Under clear instructions from Mrs Li Juan would not give the dog sweets. But Yin's intellectual capacity for clear thinking was in fact not on top at the moment.Therefore got it now to his delight out how both chewy rats and foam banana with chocolate taste. According tail increased pace tasted excellent. Did however settle for just a bit further. For then became

Yin busy with their tea. Yang, however, soon came up to her in bed. Leaning back against the wall with both legs pulled up. A newspaper on the thighs and a teacup in his right hand. The left arm around the dog affectionately sat right next.Took a sip of times while she showed the dog a newspaper photo. A beautiful color image of stars and galaxies. Read aloud to him from an article by a certain Professor Lawrence Krauss and told almost educational for the dog ...

☐   These little dots that light are stars, you understand. And ... the little more blurred and slightly larger galaxies. Giant collections of stars. Several billions even. Imagine !? And somewhere amongst all this, is our planet Earth. And on that of all the places we sit. You and I! Can you believe it, Yang ?? Just you and me ... of all.

The dog yawned wide and licked her fleetingly on the earlobe. Seemed only moderately interested. Had obviously not the same philosophy of life. Alive in the moment, and thought that was enough. And why not. Maybe it has always been man's greatest deficiency. Not being able to live in the present. Where we are actually inferior to the other animals, she thought, while the eyelids barely managed to hold himself up.

After an hour she came round again. Turned on the radio and immediately began to add up the schedule for tomorrow. While soft music flowed through the room. Took Yang in the front paws and danced with him to the beat of the music. Probably with greater desire than the dog. But still seemed not dismiss it. So why not? Got tired though after a certain time. No, this was it tomorrow instead. First they would go to the game over and try to sell the laptop. Then came there, to find a place where someone jewelers could evaluate the jewelery. Without being cheated, of course ...!? That alone is a challenge, she understood very well. Suddenly remembered that dog food was out of the bowl. While she found that fancy dog vest plastic bag. It was thin and airy. Discreet black with a faint pattern. Tried it once the dog. Perfectly suited to the brown coat. And why would not it? It was the dog's own then probably for a long time. Also had a zipped compartment on the top. Smart, thought Yin. Where one can stop into dog food. But come the moment of another use for the tray. She opened her old suitcase.Took it out there tygbyltet and opened it again. Felt the cold steel resting in his hand. Her original plan to throw the gun in the Pearl River took a completely different turn. Knew of course that it was loaded and stuffed therefore carefully into it through the zipper. Yes, the whole weapon went in through the gap and even got room inside the compartment. The zipper could also be closed. Perfect, she thought, and let the gun to remain there.Later in the evening she was freed, however, vest dog. Can not be so nice to sleep in it, she assumed. For ... it was namely the meeting with the pickpocket who founded the idea of the weapon. Namely, that the gun could be a good life. That is, if you only have it with him. Nobody knows what can happen out there among streets and alleys. Specially for a lonely young girl. But so it was only when he discovered the zipper and the union of the vest as token fell down. When the idea developed into the perfect hiding place for the weapon. No one would even be able to guess, the dog carrying around a gun. If any threatening situation arise, she quickly pick up the dog in her arms. Everything to just pretend like it needed calmed down. Once up there had the free access to the zipper and thus also to the gun. Was actually a bit proud that she came on the whole.

With the computer in a bag and Yang in his fine West came out on the street the next day. Was met by lots of rubbish lying everywhere. It was everything that the storm had emerged from their hiding places. Everything from trash bags to tree branches blown down. However, most of which were undetectable. The street looked more like after a several-day-long festival. And then not at all cleaned. They got here and tick its way between the rubble along the streets. Even so, they came to the arcade to the end. The day was slightly Yin nedklädd. It was a matter, not to look too wealthy out. Then you could hopefully negotiate a higher price. Right or wrong, but it was anyway so she thought. She then around his neck bar three very precious necklaces, nor was nothing that ought to be exposed in public. For the same reason, of course. Once up on the second floor, she saw no known among the gaming clientele. When the bandits, however, an older woman among all the young men. She definitely wanted to greet Yang. After talking with her for a while she went to the manager's door. Knocked and waited nervously. After a while, the door opened by her unknown man. Explained his case and mentioned the course of its previous business there in the office. After carefully tried the computer, he gave her a bid. Yin almost thought it was a skambud, still wanted while having it sold. Therefore took a chance and increase of a few hundred to a thousand yuan remains. Tried to look serious and definite out. As if it was her last bid ...!?

With a satisfied smile and yuan richer they left eventually gaming hall. Also stopped for a moment to hug. Yang was as happy as Yin. Despite its pyramidal ignorance about what money is. What unconcerned life dogs, she thought, and literally dragged along the pavement. With a newly appointed mistress dubious authority. Stubbornly struggling to at least try to prevent it from sniffing around every blown thing it saw. After a while they walked past a colorful fruit stand. Full of all possible gifts from Mother Earth. Not to mention the vegetables in their whole range. Yang pulled anxiously at the leash toward the solstice. Yin noted in passing a couple of older and distinguished women who stood there and picked the fruit. Ardently discussing with the dealer. Just as they passed the ladies, bit the dog while in a women's handbag was on the ground next. Went then just continue with the catch. Just as if nothing happened. One of the women discovered, however, that her bag suddenly disappeared. Probably hit it against her legs slightly. Therefore turned wondering about. Then began to also call out to attract everyone's attention. Yin, everything looked like in slow motion and did not react. Immediately understood that it would be a God's life and it was there, too. Although Yin got the dog to let go of the bag. What she immediately with an apology gave back to the lady. Still, Yin almost accused of having a real beast of a dog. Got upset Yin to understand that the bag really was not any dog bones. That she would have better pli on his bitch as the crass called. Yang looked growling long on the lady. Now, with the bag in his hand. Then gave up a will towards her. Just because she took something that he had found. Yin, however, tried to joke away the whole thing. Explained to her that it liked handbags. The indignant lady gradually calmed down and muttered something inaudible. Before she went back to their business at the fruit stand. Only when they come away from the ladies, she gave Yang a piece of candy and patted it. Was almost overwhelmed that it learned that the bags so quickly. And already proven in practice too. It bodes well for the future, she thought.

However, was so busy with the dog, she forgot what street they were on. Until they suddenly faced against him. Had more or less deliberately tried to stay away from the area around the street Nr. 119 Kengkou Rd. But there he stood right in front of them. Uncle Chen then. Yin hesitated at first but then said ...

- Ni hao!
- Ni hao! But what the hell, there you are, he said and stayed up noticeably surprised.
- Yeah, right. This is me and ... there you are.
- Did not at first recognize you. I mean, that new hair-style and everything. And a dog you also ...!? Nice little pooch! Whose is it?
- In a way, my might say. It is called Yang. Do not be afraid only. The sniffing and climbing all of which it meets. Is so kind and well-mannered.
- Well, there you see. And ... you just disappeared from the apartment and job !? Why then?
- Thanks! Yes, it's a long story. Do not know if I can tell it now? But, that night, when you left the apartment after your "little beer fest". Then you forgot to bring a certain person out. To say the least unpleasant type ad-

dition. I indeed had, to give me after ... his behavior towards me.

- Ohh hell! I had no idea. It was Luohan. Is really friend of my friend, if you say so. Well, it was like hell. Have not actually seen him since then ...!? Strangely. Just know that he is unemployed since long. Has been home with him once. Yes, we had a poker night there for some six months ago.

- Ok. But then you know that, were he lives.

- Oh yes! He lives not far from here, actually. Perhaps a hundred meters further up the street at the hardware store Li W ǔ j in N Sh A ngdi a n.

- Well, he stole something from me, and therefore I would like to meet him.

- Oh heck !? However, he was so packed when we left him. Unlike us who drank beer then. Drank the only red liquor all the time the token. Could he really do anything at all in that state ...?

- Obviously, he could it.

- Yeah. Jojo, I believe you. Do not know him closer so there. There are always those in which types everywhere.

- He lives then there above the hardware store. What's he saying?

- Luohan, he named. The surname possibly Cheung ... or something like that !? I'm not sure. But ... where do you live for yourself now?

- Luohan Cheung. I'll remember. No, I'm staying with a ... friend, you could say. We share a room. It is cheaper that way.
- Well yes, of course. Man should live too. But ... what do you do then?
- I ...?! Well ... I mug people out of money ..! No, I'm just kidding. Or not really !? I sit namely the cashier at a restaurant in town. Charge that is. Money ... you take huh ?!
- Well, sure. At checkout, that is. But, what is it for a restaurant then?
- A place where people come in and eat ...
- M etc., I understand ... No, I ... I have a little rush actually. Should namely to ... somewhere ... a turn. But like I said ... it was good to see you again. We hit well when we meet ...?! I know right?
- Well, we do safely. Take care ... and health is not the mother!
- Ha ha ha ... No, I promise! Bye dog ... hey ... hey hey.

Yin stood on the sidewalk for a long time, thinking. She had been a smoker, she lit a cigarette right then. While demanded namely a mental break. Declined slowly into some kind introverted state of meditation. Even the dog noticed. The lay namely down on the belly, despite all the potential fragrance items that passed by. Luohan Cheung, she repeated to herself. Luohan Cheung. There were many ideas that now bounced back and forth through the synapses. The exterior is not visibly affected by mental activity inside. Was just left there with eyes fixed somewhere far away in the distance. Did not even cyclists in large clusters passed by. Did not even the trucks that sometimes roared passed on the street. Often with a tail of smelly diesel fumes behind. Was no longer aware of the multitude of people who streamed past her. Was the closest to a transidental level. A condition that the easier way could be described as ... a decision anxiety. But not any decision. Rather, it was a life-changing choices that were waiting for a decision. Which she was fully aware. Hence the reluctance of her agonizing decision.The metamorphosis from the statue to an ordinary girl going somewhere was gradual. Headed eventually to a nearby shop selling fur clothing. Went in there and asked to look at some thin leather gloves. As the order took first tried the pair like a glove. They were indeed quite expensive, but the price was now of secondary importance. Paid and left satisfied out of the deal. To return to a humble note in the madding anthem.

Intoxicating vendetta

Some half an hour later, she and Yang brought in at a cafe. Was leaning back at a window table as usual. Now, with a good view of the street. A hardware store was opposite. Had been craving a cup of coffee after rekognoserat bit of a staircase right next to the hardware store. The name Luohan Chean on the board immediately caught her attention. It shone brightest among the names in the entrance. It was certainly not Cheong ... but Chean, but the difference is probably only of academic interest, she said. The painting spoke volumes. It was then where the creature lived !? What if he just knew that I now sit here on the street, she thought with an awakening hatred within themselves. Was almost about to lose control of what she is in the imagination was capable of doing. Yang was under the table and slept. Yin ordered a glass of liqueur. The waiter gave her a few options to choose from and it was orange liqueur. Sounds at least good and sweet, she thought. A relatively large glass of wine typology with orange content were developed next to the coffee. It smelled good and the taste was also on par with both the appearance and smell. However, any overheating of the palate and throat. Even the coffee tastes better now, it hit her. Along with the aftertaste of the liqueur. Barely noticed the people who passed by outside the window. Her focus was instead on the hardware store and the house where next. Unable to drop the idea of her slayer might was there. Right now even !? She enjoyed the orange-flavored beverage.Although the hot coffee solidified the burning sensation down through the throat. Even ordered a cake for himself and the dog. Split it in half and made obvious the dog's great appreciation for the idea. Is probably not accustomed to sweet cakes, but what do you do for her little darling, she thought, and sipped on the liqueur in thoughtful silence.

Some half an hour later it was developed a new glass of the same kind. In Yin's own request, of course. Perhaps orange flavor that whets the appetite, she thought, and took off his jacket. For another effect of the liqueur was that the body temperature increased. A large TV on the wall flickered and making noise all the time. It was a sort of entertainment program with too much applause and melody. Yin also asked them to lower the volume. Can not think clearly or else, she said. Blamed the dog's sensitive hearing. As the liquor dropped in the glass, she felt the irritation rose in him. Thought with disgust at that kind. Creature, as deeply into the soul humiliated her.Why should such a really allowed to go loose, she asked indignantly. His gaze became more dreamy and nailed in jail opposite. Now felt hot and slightly drunk too. But what does it matter. None at all, she thought. For now one must somehow deal with that devil. He will damn me off the hook. Swore nearly audible to the other guests. The limits of what was reasonable had already been erased with her. Now it was deeper instincts took command of her intellect. Just wait, she said, and drained the last drops in the glass. No you Yang, now let out and do justice in this stupid world. Or how Yang, she said, patting the somewhat blunt. Before they left the cafe, she asked staff for some cotton. Yes, of course I can pay for it, she slurred precariously. It did well for a minute, before a lady from the kitchen came out with a big wad. It costs nothing, 'she said and smiled sympathetically.

She walked slowly with unsteady steps past the iron trade. Unsteady she stopped outside the door to the stairwell. Peered in through the window box to re-confirm that the name was still there. And it did. Stood there for a moment. Just to come to the knowledge of, that she should have had a cigarette. Hesitated a bit but opened the door. Drew then bring the dog into the stairwell. It sniffed course around everywhere. Eager as it was. Yes, you are fine to Yang, she said, and watched with unfocused gaze down into the dog's innocent eyes. Picked up the cotton out of his pocket and bent down. Pulled apart some small balls and rolled them together into small sausages. Put two of them in Yang's ears. The other two of their own. Then took on himself the newly purchased thin and elegant leather gloves. They tightened tightly around her thin beautiful little hand. Looked back at the name board and realized that that man locomotives actually lived at the bottom of the ground floor. Went further into the corridor and soon found the door with his name. Probably well located apartment for a backyard, she thought, while Yang was lifted up from the stone floor. With the dog in his arms, with trembling hands, she called on. Noted with satisfaction that no such there was a peephole in the door. It took a while, but then opened it a little dubious and a staring eye could be seen inside the dark narrow gap.

- Hello. I am looking Luohan chean. Is it perhaps you?
- What is it?
- Well, I have a message from Chen Chiu you probably feel ... right.
- And what does he want me?
- Well, you usually supposed to play poker together sometimes ... right.
- It happens well ...
- Yes, exactly. Therefore, I have a message for you here. Can I come in?

The man showed a doubtful but slightly increasing interest and pushed open the door slightly ajar. Exposed his bearded face and unabashedly his naked hairy-chested. Then took a step back to show her that she could get into. Yin stepped over the threshold. Closed the door behind him and looked him straight in the eyes for a few seconds. Thought is now even remember the special smell from him. Felt again the hatred and vengeance desire to grow within him. Then pulled up the zipper on dog vest and put the leather-clad hand. The man, who certainly expected a patch or some kind of letter looked most surprised at the gun. It was now pointing straight at him.She was in a trance. Hardly knew whether it was he or his stepfather that she was aiming for ?! The next two, three seconds seemed like an eternity. Even until the moment when the flame and roar of the gun completely shocked both her and the dog. Dropped through the gun to the sharp rebound. Yang howled and tried to game the wriggling free. While the man fell backwards into the hall. Although Yin became self as petrified. It rang in his ears and heart rushed. Suddenly felt completely sober. The sight of the man lying motionless on the floor, got her but instinctively to get out of the shock. Now is the time to act, that she moved herself. Patted and hugged the dog to calm down, as best it was now. Picked up the gun from the floor and put it back in the slot on the vest. However, it was with doubt and worry as she carefully opened the front door from the apartment. Listened intently for any sound from the neighbors. But when the only sound was total silence, she slipped out the door and headed back toward the entrance. The legs shook under her, when she promptly made it through the corridor. Still with Yang in his arms. However, not panicked howling anymore, but intense panting with his tongue far out. Now we have to quickly get away from here, she realized. Once out on the street, she released the dog down and switched on. It was obviously very stressed out and peed right away in the middle of the sidewalk. Also reacted instinctively with a card to be against someone who just then happened to pass by. Sat down, however, and gave it a short while. All to bring down the levels of stress hormones in the poor little body. Hurried then removed from there. Must be away from here ... she repeated nervously all the way along the street.

Only a few blocks away she stopped. Out of breath and nervously watching behind her, she disappeared into the foyer of a cinema. A seedy place suitable happened to be right there. All to hide and at the same time be able to breathe for a while. The dog's breathing was still labored, and saliva dripped down on the marble floor, where they now stood. Her legs felt like a newborn calf. Sat on the safe side down on the tail. Only when she discovered her leather gloves still on her hands. Drew with some difficulty by them from their still trembling and moist hands. Yang tried to lick her face, but the air was only enough for a short wet kiss. Since it was once forced to compensate for the lack of oxygen. Puffed up and looked a little quizzical up at Yin. Got a little massage of the back, while she spoke reassuring to it. The foyer was otherwise completely deserted and no one appeared in the box office either. What Yin really appreciated in this situation. Eventually moved over to a bench a little further into the room. Just for a few paintings with movie posters. The dog jumped up beside her to seek a little security. There they sat together safely an hour or so and waited. Meanwhile, also opened the checkout. An elderly lady who, however, took no notice of them. But mostly sat there and talked on her cell phone. What if she only knew, thought Yin. Wonder what she would then do? Call the police, of course. What else !? Could not stop thinking that she would soon be the most sought after in the entire city. At least until something similar happened again. Elsewhere. But it was unlikely anyway, no one had yet found the man. Got may not visit as often either. It can at best take several weeks, she comforted themselves with. Before the creature starts to smell.

When a couple came into the foyer and bought movie tickets, she got the idea. That also disappear in there for a couple of hours. Therefore went away to the cashier and asked when the movie started. Got the answer ... that the One would start about 25 minutes. The runner ... about two and a half hours. Asked her also if the dog could come inside. When the answer was in the affirmative, she solved a ticket to the movie on One. Did not the title or what it was about. Did not care either. Just that she had come into the darkness and disappear for a while. Trying to digest what happened. The dog could lie on the chair next to and sleeping. Is probably not that there crazily movie fan, she guessed, and smiled at the thought. Or how, Yang? The dog looked wide-eyed back at her and agreed generally with everything she said. They were the best friends in the world.

It was already dark when they came out of the cinema. Even a gentle rain fell through the smog. Not anything fancy, but most continuous pouring. The few streetlights that shone, reflected in the dark wet streets. Now that Yin and the dog with heavy steps went home. Stayed however, of a lady and her mobile wok kitchen on the sidewalk. Meanwhile, with the smoke from the fire was spread a wonderful aroma of food. Something completely fulfilled both Yin and Yang noses. Had repressed hunger during the last fairly dramatic hours, but now woke up again. Especially at the sight, and the fragrant vapors from the stir-fried shredded beef, bamboo shoots and all the vegetables in the red-green mess. Asked her to get everything in a bag to take home. Even a special portion to the dog was in order. Aunt smiled constantly during cooking. Was well pleased for each new customer. Thought even a little sorry for the wet and sad little dog. Pointed complaining to the sky and the weather unreliable powers.

Back home in safety was the necklaces and the wet clothes which first went off. Yang already on the stairs shaken off the worst, got himself still a game with the towel. Dog vest and weapon were also dry. Since they could quietly devour the delicious food. Each in his own way. Yin as usual in bed, and the dog at his bowl on the floor. Both had to settle water table drink this evening. For her, a healthier alternative for a change. A remarkable evening it was. Not at all close to any one before. Having just been through something that probably is not going to forget, she realized thoughtfully, when the empty paper plate was on the bedside table. She had killed a man. A human ... echoed the thought of her. But as she used to say. She was now accustomed to always move forward in life. And did not stop with that tradition either ... after all. Instead put on the radio and selected a station that broadcast still and contemplative traditional Chinese music. Felt the need of a meditative state to be able to sleep for the night. Yang had put in the suitcase and slept already. Self she could not think of anything. Tried the dog to just live in the moment. Crawled into bed and let your body and soul disappear into the darkness under the blanket.

Woke up of Yang's safe but tangible snoring. Because of the light from the window she realized that the clock was already much. Suddenly remembered everything from yesterday. Felt so small, naked and vulnerable.Newly awake as she was there in bed. It was as if heavy clouds choked her. Bloody its own memory. You could not turn off. Wanted right then that she was a dog. Yes, but a dog who could also think ahead. Forget yesterday and live in the present. Though still future dreams remain. With tomorrow in front of him. Heavy courage Segade together with her out of bed. Prepared a little spartan tefrukost. While yang half awake lay down on his back.Yawning, stretching lazily on itself. Soon ready for a new day. Without a thought of yesterday. Yin looked enviously down at him, while she took her first sip of steaming hot tea.

After the two raised spirits with some food, it was as if the air went out of her. Did not feel like with anything. Consoled himself with some sweet treats, but remained apathetic and melancholy in any way. Suddenly knew what she wanted anymore. It was both chaos and calm in the brain at the same time. How strange it may sound. However, took the dog out on a small dutiful round the block. So that it could do, it would at the same time have the opportunity to burn off the last of stress hormones from yesterday. Once back home, she decided to take it easy for a while and just rest. Wait and wait for the hard-awakened desire. Sat in bed and slöbläddrade in some gossip magazine. The dog was standing on the floor for a moment and looked away towards the window. Thought of course that it was more fun there. But, then went back to his favorite place in the table. She read on for all the celebrities and their flashy living, to try to forget his own.

After having harvested a couple of magazines, there was suddenly an article that made her stiffen. First reflected she was not so sure of it. However, there was a statement by a Chinese pop star who made her breathless. She read verbatim ... "I was so happy when I learned of my pregnancy. Suddenly saw the world through new eyes. Did I just see the little babies and strollers, everywhere I went. The only annoying at the time was well that with nausea every other morning. And that also often sick craving strange edible things. Such as caramel and custard in my case. "

Yin could not bring himself to read another word. Either in the article or in the newspaper. Were stuck on words ... "nausea almost every morning" ...!? Surely it could not be possible ... or ..!? My thoughts immediately went back to that night in my apartment at Uncle Chen. Certainly had repressed all that, as best we could. But now it felt like reality in a creepy way came up with her. Still, however, expressed doubts that it could be that this article almost insinuated. For just that at the home of Mr. Chen had been as well not have been real. No one can conceive then, she tried to convince herself. Unfortunately not with any convincing good results. What if it still is so damn, she realized reluctantly. Slightly self-deprecating said her inner voice, that now she had not just acquired a dog. Now, perhaps, it also would get a sibling. Even without a father ...!? Which she quickly realized both his joy and horror ...!? Hopefully still a small creature of the human race, she hoped to. Just in view of one side of the genetic origin. Did not know if she should cry or scream. None of them, however, came to his expression. Just sat quietly and looked straight down towards Yang. Maybe she would soon wake up. Breathe out and liberating to realize that everything was just a dream. Could it be so? Juggled with options back and forth and tore almost bloody arm with the nail. Everything to know if she really was awake or not. Unfortunately came to the conclusion that the probability of their alertness probably never been closer to a hundred percent than now. The reality did not want to leave. The continued callous to grimace and grin to her face. Now seemed to be caught in a trap ...!?

The concern did not want to leave her alone. Felt soon forced to reconsider their decision to stay home. Could not just sit there. Twisting and turning on the problems endlessly. No, she must be out of town and get perspective on life. Clear the brain simply. Brought Yang out of the shower room. It sat there and looked at her, while she carefully washed both hair and entire body. Felt impure in any way. Back at the apartment, she took out the gray jumpsuit. However, left his jacket in favor of the fur jacket. Would now dress up simply. Perhaps it could make her forget and move on. At least for the day ...!? Will try to return to my business, she thought, and took out of the bottomless blue fabric bag. Upholstered even in one of the handbags in the side compartment. Took on one of the treasures of necklaces. Painted easily and sprinkled even a few drops of the upscale perfume. Before she and the dog left the apartment. Had not yet brought Yang down into the subway. Nor been in the city center with him. It would be about to change now. It should be a part of it all, she thought. And is it something that it does not like, it may learn.

She brought the blue bag was not because of lack of cash, but most of the adventure and to be able to forget yesterday's trauma. It was the sheer exhilaration and excitement that attracted the most. As climbing the high mountains that comparison. To try to reach the top and to also make it on their own. In addition, there were of course here a possible reward icing on the cake. Maybe not quite unimportant factor.

But, to go to the train station, she had neither the time nor the inclination to. Instead, she happened to run into a department store. Namely Zhicheng Store. Pretty close Donghaoyong E. Rd. Not nearly as big as China Plaza, yet tastefully and elegantly decorated. Almost in English colonial style. Also there was a lot of people in motion. Many people like herself relatively classic well-dressed. Was thus in line with the environment, you could say. To her delight, she discovered that the store had a kind of elevator, where the doors are missing. Two holes in the wall next to each other. In which one contained an elevator on the way up and the other one on the way down. Continuously slowly moving words. They were, in other words jump on and off on the fly. This thought Yin was downright playground. She stepped on, went around and hopped on and off everywhere. Mostly just for fun of course. All this contained the exciting moments. Which she often searched. Such was her personality. Yang did not, however, the pleasure, without hesitation every time they would get on. Stepped finally the top of the store. Where they sold electric shavers, hairdryers and similar things. Slowly walked around the department for a while and slötittade on supply. Received after awhile view of a so-called long nose at one checkout. Yes, therefore, a man who was not Chinese but from the West somewhere. Maybe even a tourist or businessman. Which were of less interest right now. Yin received namely see the man stuffed paper bag which stood a little lonely for himself. Right diagonally behind him. As you could see, there were already more wrapped packages in it. Plus, the cashier was just about to enter one more for him. He was currently the most concentrated on his wallet and his debit card was picked up and down. Approached him mainly for reconnaissance, but realized instead that moment probably could not be better. Sometimes it was a question to act quickly. Do not hesitate too long.

With your left hand on the leash, she held Yang distance. With the second she placed carefully into the bag over the paper bag. Controlled however, all the time in which direction his attention was directed. Was actually a bit hard to get a grip on the bag two handles but failed at the last moment. Lifted it all so quietly as possible and walked away. Without even looking around. Heart pounded hard, and she felt her legs began to tremble. Just as yesterday. After some twenty meters she turned, however, to the left between a few stands and then disappeared in the crowd. Stepped gradually in the downward lift. Hann just in because of the dog that literally got pulled on board. Once down in the ground floor provided herself with a large paper bag at the checkout. Then walked out of the store. Was simultaneously re just one of the others in the crowd. Loaded the packages into the new bag. Also felt that fur jacket probably should have been left at home. Namely sweated profusely while the elegant purple blouse uncomfortable sticking themselves to the skin. Stood for a moment and took his jacket off. All to let the light wind fanning the blouse dry. In all cases no less wet. Despite the external circumstances, she felt still an inner satisfaction with the day's catch. Breathed satisfied in the relatively cooler air in the street. A relief to get out in the open. And as soon as possible to be able to go away from the crime scene, so to speak. Which she did. Lagging an empty bag and a large bag. And a dog who willingly took the whole burden by themselves.Curious tacking and sniffing of all oncoming along the sidewalk.

Strange, she thought suddenly! Today I do not feel any nausea at all. Amidst the throng and din of traffic noise made it unpleasant reminder. There may not be any children in there at all, she said ... again some hopeful !?But did anyway in the subconscious, the odds probably were not on her side. Mostly because of their periods have not been to visit for quite some time. Had not thought about it much before. Unpleasant things disappear, you notice more often than not. In addition, she had a poor concept of time in general. For example, could not work out how many weeks she had been in Guangzhou. Most perhaps because she really did not care. Time passes and I with it, she considered crass. On the way to Beijing Road, she happened to pass an LBX Pharmacy. A pharmacy chain that is everywhere in China. Stopped for a moment, thinking. Adopted namely, that there should be pregnancy tests to buy. There, if anywhere, she thought, and went in through the revolving door. With some hesitation and apparent shame she went, however, and asked. It was found that they had several different types. Yin bought however the cheapest one for 29 yuan. The girl at the pharmacy explained how to do. Seemed surprisingly simple, she thought. Just a kind of urine. How hard could it be? However, there was not really any great expectation of the outcome. Quite the contrary. But ... not knowing ... I felt even worse.

She had previously seen many exclusive stores selling watches and jewelry on Beijing Road. Searched therefore up one of them. Namely wanted to get her necklace valued. Whether it was now the real thing. Both the stone and chain. The man behind the counter bowed politely to her. Looked down on Yin through his thick glasses and spoke to her as if she were a little schoolgirl. Not even when she took out the necklace, he changed his paternal attitude. Even greeted the dog and spoke to it in just the same way ...!? Then turned back towards Yin ...

- Let's see here, he said, and took the pendant in his hand. Have you bought it yourself or is it an heirloom?
- No, I got it from ... my aunt ... who died. A while ago ...
- A patrimony that is. Well, then we'll take a closer look at it. Should only download a device.

He disappeared behind a curtain and Yin took the opportunity to look around among all the treasures behind glass doors. Considering the price tag of amount, it is probably no farmers from land that is here, she thought. The man came right back with a cardboard box in his hand. However, took only a microscope and examined the chain ...

- It is silver, I see directly on the stamp here.
- Yes, that was probably it, I thought.
- As for these three large polished stones in the pendant, I'll just check one thing first.

The man brought the stones to the mouth and breathed a long time for them. Then he quickly took the magnifying glass and looked at the stones. Repeating the procedure on each stone and said ...

- For I would see how quickly the water vapor evaporates from the stone.
- Well ...!?
- Well, that's just, I have time to see it. But it evaporates so quickly is a good sign.
- OOPS!

Then he went to the instrument. A black thing with wires and a few shining lights in a row. Measured the one stone at a time. The lights blinked and shone. Even a beep came occasionally.

- You then had received it after your aunt. Did you get a number like this jewelry?
- Hmmm ... well, I have a necklace to home. But it does not look exactly the same.
- I can at least tell you that all three of the stones are cut brilliants. Of exquisite quality in addition. I can see in the microscope if nothing else. There are some irregular structures inside them and it should be in genuine stones. Or rather ... it is only in genuine they are.
- Brilliants ... ?? What is it? Is it valuable stones?
- Joo, little lady. Diamonds are genuine faceted diamonds. In this case also of very high quality.
- Diamonds then ...!?!
- Yeah. Really!
- But ... oh well. Well ... ahh ...
- Did you perhaps planning to sell the necklace?

- Joo. Maybe ... I think in any case. But, however much it may be worth then?

- Yes, it depends on which buyers can find. But if I grossly would estimate the value of the market, so ... I guess about ... 150 to 200 ... million yuan, my dear!

- 200 thousand yuan ...!?!

- Well, in any case, at least ... 150. At the right buyer, that is.

- Where can you sell it then?

- Yes, sometimes we also buys jewelry. But when it comes to this kind of quality merchandise, I would recommend an auction. One of them is not so far from here. A little further down on this street. The units Nanfang Pāimài. There you can submit items that are then sold at the next auction. You can set a minimum price, if you want ... of course.

- How often has that ... auction ... then?

- That depends. It switches namely theme. One time it might be art. Next antiques or as in your case ... for example, jewelry. It is best that you go there and ask yourself. OK ...?!

- Thanks! How well. Then I will do it. Ahh ... what does this now?

- No, we take no for valuation. But, if you get it sold so please come here and buy something else. There are many great works of art in the form of jewelry and watches. You are so welcome!

- Thank you, I will really remember ... in that case.

Yin left the store with his mouth formed a smile. Right now felt all the problems almost forgotten. At least for the rest of the day. One hundred and fifty thousand yuan !! The thought of all the money spun around inside the black bangs. It was an unimaginable sum for her. Not to mention how mother would experience the amount, she thought. However, she should really get some of the money. If I get the necklace sold to say? Just wait for Mom! Once you move away from that worn in tobacco plants and preferably also your emetics to be. Soon, so ...!? Yin had received directions to Nan-fang Pāimài of the man in the store and was now on his way there.However, then came the tiredness suddenly over her. Therefore thought that it would be ideal to relax with an ice cream. Passed timely Shun and slipped in there to buy a durian ice cream. A yellow creation shaped like an egg. Served in plastic film by any reason. Took the ice cream and sat down on a bench to rest a while. The wooden bench was a total of four in a square surrounded a thick old trees. In the middle of the pedestrian Beijing Road. Like tree formations, she saw several places farther away. Sat and fanned themselves, while people strolled past her at a leisurely pace. Many of them were young couples hand in hand. Felt like a small thorn in the heart. A feeling of being excluded from the community. Although uncertainty whether she really wanted to be with someone, also confused her. Did not really what she wanted. Always had the feeling of pushing life ahead of him. As if there were always more important things first tackle. Then ... starting life itself, she had imagined. Yang also got a little taste of the ice cream. Especially the one that flowed down along one finger. Both she and the dog enjoyed the sweet and good snack. While a woman with a baby carriage came towards them. Then swept re unrest clouds down over existence. Each stroller a premonition, what might come forward. However, tried to quickly push back the idea and instead just focus on the necklace and that the auction firm.

Barely half an hour later she stood inside the auction house Nanfang Pāimài. The decor felt exclusive and closest beautifully antique in any way. Showed their jewelry and discussed with the staff about appropriate next auction. After a quick assessment she was told that her jewelry would fit on the next appropriate clearance. That is, if quite exactly two weeks. She accepted the proposal and left both the necklace and his address there.Received in exchange for an elegant receipt which was first signed in duplicate. One of the selling party and the other for the auction agency's behalf. Yin felt both safe and satisfied. For they had agreed on a limit of 140 000 yuan. If no bid above the price arrived, she got to keep it. For sales took firm seven percent commission on the sale amount. It said Yin was reasonable. Especially considering what it had cost her ... in the purchase ...!? She did Nanfang Pāimài quite satisfied and especially excited. If only a few weeks she would know ...!? Naturally also self presently there in the audience at the auction day. Which she looked forward.

Had been sitting all the way home on the subway and almost only thought about money. What you could do for them all. She could, for example moving to another apartment and ... yes, there was how much anywhere ...!? It was not until she would get off as it suddenly dawned on her. Bag with packets ...!? Where is the bag, she thought, slightly panic? For some reason she looked about the caravan. But realized understood immediately that she had forgotten it somewhere. I fucking forgot the bag, she said bluntly. A woman opposite looked at her in surprise. Shortly thereafter slowed the train. She arrived at the final stop and went sullen by train. Stared straight ahead. Went anxiously for a ride on the platform before she sat down on the only available was there. A cold stone sofa. Did admittedly cold in the butt, but the brain however went hot all the thoughts that just spun around. Where was the bag? In memory flushed her back everything that had happened the last hours in the city. Felt too shocked to really remember anything. Unfortunately, she felt almost sure that the bag was not even inside the auction house. To her disappointment, she realized then, that in principle it could be anywhere. So somewhere between the store and the auction firm. Hopelessness drug that a cold wind through her. The prospect of seeing it again is not large, she realized. Furthermore, less and less the longer you think about it. But, as they say. I had nothing when I came. That is to say, when I went into town. You have to look at it that way, she thought. Despite the still somewhat resignedly. Kudos to the person who found it. Sour, it was. But of course, no more acidic than it most likely would have been the man in the store. Now she got himself playing the victim role. However, probably no lesson that would put some long track. Was in fact too targeted to be discouraged by adversity. Or more ...? Which would also be proven.

Remained seated on the cold and rock hard couch for a while longer. Felt a little off and melancholy. Almost like when you have been wronged. Also thought that pregnancy tests. Not at all something that attracted her. But of course, she thought. Would it be a positive "non pregnant" answer, it would seem like a lottery win. While understanding that any luck, she had never had. However, it could shit themselves, she tried a little humorous. Yang had luckily not the problems. Instead, it began now pulling on the leash. As if it wanted to go anywhere. Yin was however back all the time, but was eventually forced to look for. What was it that attracted him ?! Saw only the back of a dozen people waiting on the other side of the platform. Apparently waiting for the next train into town. Discovered, however, an older elegant woman who was more behind the other. Fully concentrated on make-up with small mirror in front of your nose. Tried to improve the few parts of the face that still had the possibility remains. Right next to the lady on the platform were the cause of the dog's desire. There stood namely a purse. The makeup spirit lady handsome thing in patterned black glossy leather. Yin considered the situation a few seconds, but then took a quick decision. Unhitched the dog from the leash and let it away. The dog's earlier zeal slowed slightly. Instead, it went with little mincing steps toward the lady. Just as it had learned. Took quite inconspicuous bag in his mouth and turned on. Without a sound, and perhaps even without anyone seen it all. Trotted nicely back towards Yin himself quickly stood up and left the platform. Towards the end, and then up the stairs. With the dog just behind. However did not stop until the street level. First, where she turned around and gave Yang. The released however grudgingly and a little growl from the bag. Only after bribed with a candy bar. The purse disappeared quickly under the blue bag. Whereupon they calmly walked from there through a stationary light rain. In the direction of home with the dog feedback. Via a carriage borne wokställe where a portion of the hot fuming chicken noodles were taken into a bag.

After the meal could Yin not decide what she would do first. Open purse or do pregnancy tests. It was, however, the latter option. If one then possibly have to console themselves, the inventory of the handbag an alternative, she thought. Yang slurped itself the last remains of the wok, while Yin went out to the toilet for the urine sample. Followed instructions carefully and were also waiting the specified time before the final results could be read.The minutes crawled. Did not even know if she dared to look at that dipstick. Felt so vital in any way. Like standing at a crossroads, and neither know here or there. The election would now fate instead do about her. Had certainly heard of abortion ...!? But then it may not be too late, what she did ?! Meanwhile, it seemed that option so cruel. Moreover, she was deathly afraid of hospitals, doctors and all that. So ... just that opportunity seemed too distant ... unfortunately.

The decisive moment had come. She almost closed her eyes when the stick was removed from the sample. Had read the operating instructions and knew exactly how the response options appeared. That is to say, what one or the other meant to her. Still took courage to himself and looked. The second lasted an eternity. Eyes immediately took in the result, but the brain did not hang with. Then looked for a long while to convince himself ...

- I knew it, she cried loudly. I fucking knew it, she went on a couple more times.
- Djäkla shit too! Damn ...
- I think I die ...
- Mom, can you hear me? ! I'll have a baby ...!
- A child ... mother ...
- Well ...!? Well, it went for me .... Thank you for the pass.

Since the stick in despair thrown on the floor, she threw herself on the bed and just ... cried. Let the tears flow out of the eye. Sobbed and Oxfords. Yang wondered understood and realized, too, that something was not as it should. Skipped therefore up to her in bed. Licked clean her salty tears on his cheeks and chin. A little mascara and snot slipped safe also. But what did it matter. Dogs are not so discerning and certainly not some gourmets directly. They can put itself worse things than that. Which previously also been proven. It then lay close to her. Watched with wide eyes into her own sticky and bloodshot. Probably tried to comfort her and himself. A kind of win-win situation, you might say.

Only a few hours later she came to think of it, where the purse. It was still standing inside the door. At that time, all the tears secreted amounts of calming hormones. Although she felt listless, started brain to recover. At least to a more normal level. Turned on the radio. Remained for a while in bed, while she tenderly stroked contented Yang over the soft fur. Back and forth. The touch was like a kind of therapy for her. A healing balm for the aching heart. Estimated that the dog was now in her. Not having to be completely alone with their thoughts. Spinning around in the skull. Crawled still out of bed and picked up the purse. It not only shone in quality but also surrounded by a wonderful scent. Probably a string of lady's perfume, she assumed. The pattern of the beautiful leather looked like crocodile skin, but it certainly was not. The opening mechanism on the other hand was perhaps more of the real thing. Saw anyway like gold. At least gulddoublé. There she was sure. This time she went more rational approach. Turned simply up and down on the bag. Out over the blanket fell both the one and the other. Everything from the ordinary paper tissues to a black alluring shiny mobile phone. Only it is worth the effort, she thought, and continued the inventory of the content. Found including a wallet with more than two hundred yuan in cash. Even a few credit cards in the same. These, however, were thrown down immediately among wokkartonger and other debris in the small trash can by the bed. A small bottle of eau de toilette also appeared on order. So it was from there that the smell originated. There she realized after having sprayed a shower on the wrist. The bottle, she would certainly

keep. The rest were mostly uninteresting rubbish. Which also relegated to the basket. The bag itself,
however, she put on the bedside table. Perhaps the
most to admire. Knew not what it was worth, or what
she really would have it. After an evening walk with the
dog in the streets escalated, she eventually dropped for
the day and went to bed. With soft music from the radio
mellowed soon the grim indeed a refreshing dream.

The whole next day disappeared with practical issues
here and there. Not until darkness had again descended
on the town, she went off to the girls at the factory
site. Now they know. Might as well say that it is, she
thought.Needed comfort from more than Yang. When
she made her entrance in the small bedroom, she could
only see two of them. But the more excited they became,
when she suddenly appeared from nowhere. And ...
when they saw the dog, almost cheered the happiness. Threw himself down on the floor and greeted
Yang was panting with excitement tried to lick them
everywhere.

- Hey by the way! Is that your dog?
- Well, now at least. Got to take over from an older man
who became ill.
- Really !? What sweet it is. What's that?
- Yang!
- What a funny name. Hey, Yang ...

- It's very clever. Was actually there, even when I got it. However, I have been training a bit with it too. Is my best friend now. It is he and I, making you ...!? Do not need another guy that is.
- Ha ha ha, I understand. Really. But by the way, how is it else where?
- Joo, I thought, well get to it, but where are the other girls?
- They work over. Probably all night, I would guess. We escaped. At least tonight in all cases. Phew!
- Aha ...! Well, I can understand that. Well, as I said ...

Then she told me all about the pregnancy for them. If the test that she had done and about their own thoughts about the whole story. However, not a word about their incredible movements in which brute Luohans apartment.It would remain a secret, so long as she lived. So it was decided. Unless she would be unmasked and arrested, ie. Though this option was not even in her imagination. Showed them also the "new" cell phone. Claimed that she found it on a couch inside Beijing Road. The girls who had themselves respectively, recommended her to take out the SIM card and then purchase a prepaid card instead. Yin was quite a novice in the area were advised therefore to visit a phone shop. However, they picked out the SIM card for her. Then they programmed into their own number in the phone. So she could call them whenever she wanted. Yin was so grateful for the help. Ran even out to a convenience store and bought some delicious cakes to kvällstéet. At last she would be able to communicate via their own mobile. Not only see all the other walking around and talking in these matters star. The time the girls went as usual everything too fast. Yet they managed to gossip about everything. Both serious and hilarious units discussed during evening coffee break and the rest of the evening. Yang had never been so omsvärmad. Which tail unless otherwise expressed. Before she left, promised both decided that the girls would always be there for her. If she wanted to have the support then? After a rewarding and enjoyable evening did they eventually say goodbye to each other, and she left their spartan shelter with a sense of confidence. The hope of life after all. Even in the seat that fate now set her in.

The mistake ödestigra

Days passed and was soon to weeks. One noticed now, that evenings have become slightly cooler. But chillier in Guangzhou does not mean that it is cold. Just that you might have to put on a jacket or sweater for the evening. Yin however, it was just a favor. Then she could make better use of their fur jacket over his increasingly frequent evening visits inside the city. For it was then and there that she and the people there certainly lived up. One strolling around among neonljusens iridescence. Ate and shopped alternately. Talked, laughed and simply enjoyed the pleasant urban togetherness. Especially in the pedestrian streets where no cars could destroy the calm and convivial atmosphere. That January soon began to draw to a close, saw the number of wrapped packages that many wore on. For the New Year celebrations in the end of the month went to many of the townspeople back to their home areas. For after days long trips in crowded trains greet their loved ones. At least once a year. Such is the tradition in China and even the economic revolution can probably change it. One just home quite easily. Cost what it wants. Despite a return to the often snow-covered villages and icy cities. For chilly houses and apartments where the most is the New Year celebrations which will be borne warming. Besides the warm reunion of his parents and siblings of course. This is the time that most Chinese people look forward with pleasure and anticipation. Despite all the hardships during queuing at the train stations and the congestion in the overcrowded trains and buses. Most sleeping through the long journeys. No matter what uncomfortable position as they are forced to spend time. Among all its equally uncomfortable road users.

Yin had no intention to return home over the New Year. Especially not in the situation she was in. The information she thought not communicate it to them at home. Certainly not at the moment anyway. Her supposed pregnancy had now also been confirmed by a doctor in addition. So she must come to terms with his fate. While it can often seem unfair and inconvenient, she thought. That life ahead summer would completely change her life, she was quite clear about. Although it fully impossible to imagine, had yet to process the reality already started. If not yet on a large scale. However, her theft raids with the blue bag borne more fruit. Even the dog had been routine at that downloading handbags. It was also how she made a living nowadays. So harsh were the circumstances. But was thankfully not possessed by any moral qualms. Which obviously facilitated it. In other words ... she slept well at night. Which even Yang did of course. However, perhaps the most because the concept of morality does not exist in the animal world. How easily can a dog get away that problem. And it seemed to also enjoy. Unconcerned and often sleeping in the red suitcase under the table. That is, when they were out on their joint and active adventure in the big city hubbub. Always a loyal soldier and caring companion. Now an indispensable part of her heart, she realized.

She called occasionally to his friends from the factory time. Sometimes they met also to snack on something nice place in town. And who paid unless she understood. In addition, always had so much to talk about. Life had almost just begun for them and their dreams for the future were discussed, therefore, with great enthusiasm and expectation. The time at the factory, they saw only as a parenthesis in life. There was so much else there.Things and events just waiting for them. It was the most confident. Although Yin obviously was marked by its own predictable next time. Held anyway courage up and shared future dreams with the girls. For none of them knew what the fate had in store. That life's critical crossroads too much influenced by chance. It was they understand. Still, it felt as if they ruled direction. One moment satisfying and comforting conviction probably. Yin wondered myself often that by chance. So many random events that so far pushed them further through the mazes of fate. Just then her that day passed the city limits to Guangzhou. Some she remembered with a smile, while others gave her anxiety. It is as if things just to happen, she thought. As necessary links in a long chain of events. Yet relatively satisfied with life compared to his previous home on the farm. Where was the word future just a chimera. Identical days that followed one another until death came as a relief. Anything more useless, she could not imagine. It was also precisely why she was here in the middle of the action. A place where every step could take a new and unpredictable directions and scenarios. A place where life could be lived, so to speak. Perhaps for good and bad ... but still. Was it something you regretted, it could perhaps change the day after. At least for the most part. However, you could of course not give any life back. Now if you should happen to want it ...!?

A setback that still weighed on her, however, to the elegant necklace had not been sold at the auction. It grieved her almost every day. Even so, she had let the jewelry go to the next appropriate auction. However, the first few weeks inside the new year. One day she did not want to think too much. The disappointment was in fact much stronger than the feeling at success. She had learned during this time in the big city. Where happiness is actually often been her companion. Yet she could not rejoice fully at these times. Not even when, as expected appeared. Gloom was somehow more a normal state with her. Probably a relic from his past. What did she know?

Both stood in the crowding of the New Year's travelers at the eastern railway station. It was the Yin and the artistic Da Xia from the factory. They waited for her kvällståg would soon come in Track 1. She was on her way home to her parents and her younger sister to celebrate New Year. A long and tiring journey on the full 22 hours. Yin had invited her on taxi to get there and where most of that friend and companion in anticipation of retirement. Had also helped her with the packing until the platform. Remember, you must be a mother, suddenly said Da Xia almost envy in his voice. Yin sigh most wanted and quickly change the subject. Pointing out instead that it was lucky, that Yang had to be left in the factory apartment. The noise level in the hall was namely deafening with all the people talking to each other. In addition, also in the mouth on the raspy lady in the speaker constantly informed passengers about times and trains in a mix. Exactly what ... you could not hear. Was instead forced to rely on their own vision and hearing. They really make an effort to pacify his place in the crowd. Then, when the delayed train after a half hour slipped in along the platform, erupted sheer uproar. All would be understood in the train at the same time. It was jungle in force. Suitcases, backpacks and other loose goods suddenly turned into weapons in the battle for a place in the train. The word respect pretended not to have heard before. One would board at any price. Yin helped Da Xia to pave the way through the crowd. It was obviously better if they were two. Yin acted as battering ram in front to clear the way for her friend. Which also proved to produce results. With a bit of luck and with the help of the crowd pressure from behind, of course. They ended namely right at the step up to one of the doors. It was just that they had time to say goodbye to each other, before Da Xia simply forced into the train. Luckily, with their bags in with him. A grateful glance and a brief wink was the last Yin could see of her. Then it was just to add to the slopes. Try to focus on getting away from the platform something so when safe and sound.

It was only in the taxi on the way to retrieve the dog as she felt the pain in his back and arms. Of all the bumps and blows from the battle at the station. But it was worth it, she thought. Can you help a friend in need, so will it cost. It's that simple. About Da Xia's fate and adventure in the train wagon during the long and strenuous journey, she could only speculate. Hardly would she be rocked to SOMS reclining in a comfortable and soft leather chair. In other words, quite far from the first grade on the Orient Express. Nor is fed with a spoon of stylish English butler in adequate attire. No, rather, was there, trying to sleep through suffering. With the body in the position as the surroundings of the moment allowed. The taxi ended up in a traffic jam and Yin looked suspiciously at the taximeter. The amount strode forward, even when the car is standing still. But perhaps it should be, she thought, and leaned back again. While she hauled a large white purse with key lock from his pocket. Opened and the contents turned out to consist of a number of coins and some banknotes. Nothing, actually. Counted out the money and got it to about 185 yuan. Always something, she thought, and stuffed it in his pocket again. Mildly without any scruples. She in the crowd so vigilant managed to snatch a purse from the pocket of a poor traveler, it touched her barely. It was considered rather only as "business as usuall." While the taxi was waiting, she quickly retrieved the dog. Back from the temporary dog guard in the factory apartment. One of the girls lined up a few hours before she could pull away. Back home in the taxi again, she took without hesitation the white purse and paid. The taxi ride was thus regarded as entirely self-financed. With bonus addition. Something Yin always got a kick out of.

Although there were still people left on the streets, there was a clear reduction towards normal. Now for the upcoming New Year celebrations. In a way, just nice, thought Yin. It was another quiet of the city. A time for contemplation and reflection. Something which she also used. Daily strolled around with the dog inside the core area of Guangzhou and pondered. Tried with the best ability to put the unpleasant events behind and instead look ahead. A future where admittedly only the outline could be discerned. Even if a beacon sometimes flashed far away. A kind of acknowledgment on the right course ... maybe. Decided nevertheless to further concentrate on the present. That's to come later, anyway eventually. No point in wasting energy on it. In other words, better to continue life as usual. At least for a while.

The weekend went too fast. Despite the bad weather. Suddenly it was already Monday. Had just stopped a taxi and were now heading into the city center. The umpteenth time she did not even yourself. For it was there that she usually drove his days now. Felt somehow more confident with it where intense city life. The mix of all kinds of people who beblandades. Today usually also bearing on the blue fabric bag over his shoulder and with Yang hauling the leash. Had recently visited a special mall with more or less exclusive small shops. So the idea was also today. The number of visitors was the surprising number considering New Year's leave. But of course, the proportion of residents who no longer have any relatives in the country increases, of course. More and more generations remain namely townspeople.
She wore the day a newly acquired black jacket and a pair of bright chinos. Together with brown boat

shoes. Around his neck the other of the two exclusive necklaces. Ie, that which was not yet submitted to the auction firm. Thus, quite properly dressed to be on a Monday. Took a light lunch in a nice place with a nice view of the street life. Sat there for a long while afterwards and enjoyed a cup of strong coffee and cake to. Had no direct plans for the day, but let fate control their further wanderings through the urban landscape.

Just down the road from the mall, she happened to pass by one shop. With a variety of eyeglass frames on walls and spin stands. Everything is exposed in a white almost blinding light. Almost uncomfortable, thought Yin was about to pass by. When she saw a beautiful lady about to try out a few bows. Matching her dainty face and close-cropped black hair. However, it was not the lady in question that caught Yin's interest. But rather her elegant briefcase standing next to the floor. Almost slightly too much for himself, considered Yin. Dragged the dog into the store. Began there, too yourself to try some arches from the range. Mainly for show, of course. Saw in the corner of the eye through the mirrors, the staff were busy with other customers. Both in cash and in the examination room. The sophisticated lady was still fully concentrated on his own revelation in the mirrors. All the while, she alternated between the various shelves. Sometimes almost frightening far from the portfolio addition. Which also was what Yin instinctively had anticipated. And ... at exactly the right moment put Yin down his blue bag over the portfolio. Grabbed the handle through the gap on tygväskans zipper and slid slowly out of the store. With Yang first as usual. So far everything went well. Until she was on the way out unexpectedly met his gaze from the two guards who stood leaning against a railing further out into the room. Unfortunately, with full visibility into the store. Yin felt his heart beat a somersault in his chest. Even so, she tried to stagger on as naturally as possible. However, saw all too clearly in the corner of his eye, how the guards suddenly left their seats at the railing. Divined now that the haunting tour just played out the last card. No, no, she thought. It may not be true. Surely it can not be this, it should stop ?! For it was just so far she had time to think, before a powerful hand was laid on her shoulder. Even the dog was just as surprised. It was not even to bark. Instead began curiously to sniff at the guards' legs. People like people.

- Excuse little lady, but you can put down your bag on the floor. We would like to look in the ...!?
- Why, then ... then?
- As I said, we just want to look in your bag. Do you have something inappropriate there, or ...?
- No, I have not. Also, I have not the time. Have namely a taxi waiting for me outside.

- Then it can wait a little longer. Set down your bag immediately!
- Yes, yes ... I just do not ...
- I think, on the contrary, you understand. I know right ...?

Yin remained speechless and forced to capitulate to their superiors. Put down the blue bag on the floor. Had since namely supposed to run away, but one of the guards stood in the way. While the other pulled apart the zipper and took up the portfolio. Then he went up and down on the fabric bag and held it up in front of him in both hands. Staring at Yin through the bottomless things rock and asked ...

- Do you walk around with bags without bottom?
- Well, so what then ?!
- To protect the portfolio then maybe ...
- Exactly!
- Please come with us into the store as you came out of. There, we can ask if there possibly are someone who recognizes this portfolio.
- Oh well ..?

They took the Yin to the optician, I met a surprised woman wondered what on earth they did to her portfolio. They immediately got their well-founded suspicions of the portfolio origin verified by the lady. Praise and gratitude from her almost drowned them. Unlike looks as Yin had to settle. Some darker eyes than the lady she had never seen ...!? The security officers took the woman's name and address for further interrogation and white spirit.

- You are hereby under arrest while waiting for police. Is that your own dog or have you taken it too?
- Certainly not! Yes, that is my dog. It makes you damn 'in me not to.
- We'll see, when the police arrived. Turn on you, so that we can put on the handcuffs.
- What? Handcuffs ... ??
- Such here, you understand. They are namely the small thieves like you. So you can keep your hands to ... your little monkey.

After ten minutes, she was taken away by two policemen to a waiting car outside the mall. It was hot and the car had no air conditioning. Together with a report containing witness statements from the lady and the guards, she was taken to a local police office. Where picked first of her jewelry, keys and wallet. Fabric bag was taken care of as proof equipment. Then they took her fingerprints by using black ink on your fingers. After that, she was temporarily in a cell in the basement awaiting interrogation. Luckily, along with his dog. As, however, in motstats against Yin, at least provided with a bowl of water. They appear in all cases, be animal friends here, she thought, and embraced a puzzled and uncomprehending Yang. Then settled with him in a corner of the crisp and cold cement floor. Here it is in any case not as hot as in the car, she comforted themselves with. That they had not ended up on some kind of luxury, she became every minute more and more aware. So it was like this, it would stop. Grieved and cursed his own carelessness. Unable to forgive himself. How clumsy can you be? But now she sat there. In the so-called "splendid isolation" and knew neither in or out. Could not even think of what would then happen. How she, for example, would lay out the text at the next hearing ...?! It was the most that sustained her thoughts. Ever since that nasty sound of the gates as rudely slammed behind them. Good thing the mother did not see me now, she comforted themselves with. Could then not quite free himself from the thoughts of those back home. Reflections ground in the head. Come, then suddenly thought of Da Xia. How miserable and crowded she had it on the train, it was nothing compared to this. Had even felt sorry for her there at the station. Now she got instead feel sorry for himself. If BOOB now sitting here on the rock hard floor in semi-darkness bitterly regretting it. Would gladly have traded with Da-Xia right now. She also was pregnant, did not make things easier. Realized to their sorrow that it was probably the greed that felled her. A confident jaguar hunting. And for a moment forgot to look around. The image of the metaphor burned itself into my head. The question was, how long it would continue to torment her. One of the issues that currently do not receive any reply.

The time 17:35. Hearing of Miss Yin Woo, 17 years old, on suspicion of theft on the mall Wanda Plaza. No identity documents found on the suspect. Residential Address hitherto unknown. Well ... Miss Woo ... recognize you, that you today resorted to a portfolio from an elderly lady at the Wanda Plaza Optician Service ...?

- No ... yes ... so what resorted ??
- You simply have stolen a briefcase from the current lady. Do you have difficulty understanding?
- No, not usually anyway.
- Well ... ??
- Well, what the hell ... ok then. It just happened to be so. Was hungry and had nothing to buy food.
- But ... from what I understand of visitation papers, you had the 75 yuan in a white purse and 400 in another kind of wallet ...!?
- Yes, but ... I ... I ... was to save for a trip home ... and ... did not take some of the savings money.
- What are you working with Miss Woo?
- Have not found a job yet. It is not so easy ... in fact.
- Where do you live then?

- Where I usually put my backpack ...!? Thus, it was a joke. Ok ..? No, we usually always find some place the dog and me. Otherwise, we tend to warm each other in a staircase or so.
- No fixed abode then ..? How long have you been here in Guangzhou?
- It is not so long ... actually. We came here maybe ... a few weeks ago ... Only.
- We found this business card in your wallet, Miss Woo. It has belonged to Madame Biyu Choi Hardy. With the title of Chairman of the Board of a company called Canton divertissement. In what way do you know her?
- That's right ... she ?! She ... I have worked in a while. Of ... well on her firm words.
- But, you are told you just now that you had not found a job.
- Joo sure, but ... since I stopped with her ... I mean, I have not found anything ...
- You make no credible impression so far, Miss Woo. Would ... would this lady on the business card in that case be able to identify you?
- Absolutely! She said, that ... absolutely ... could she. Call her and say ... that Yin sitting here ... and ... yes ...
- The time is 17.45. We will pause and cancel the hearing.

Yin took a slight sigh, while the interrogator and his female assistant left the room. Assumed they would now try to contact Madame. Just wondering how she will react, thought Yin. I mean, that now sits in the police.Suspected ... and so on. What she remembered, had Madame said, that if she wanted help with anything, so ......!? But this by sitting in the jail's something completely different. Can even say that she does not even know me.The tanks were dancing on thin ice. You never knew if or when logic would burst. After the hearing, she was rudely back to the cell in the basement. Realizing that her black blazer would not be hot enough down there.Clutching therefore on Yang to get a little more warmth and stroked it lightly over the coat on the head. At the same time she prayed a prayer. Which she never did before. Considered that now was needed all the help you could get. No matter where it came from. Looked reluctantly down on the gray and depressing cement floor and a shudder went through the body. A confirmation of awareness of which diabolically repulsive place she landed on. One moment like a tiny lady in paradise and now suddenly here. As a simple thief by the authorities nedsparkad and relegated to the humiliation damp cellar. As a welcome companion to cockroaches and other insects freely housed bearing on floors, walls and ceilings. Locked down in this stone gate entrance to hell. If you still wore fur jacket, she thought, and regretted his kavajval. Well, that was then this man would eventually end up. Tears filled the eyes of the width and reluctantly horrified rolled down toward the gritty stone floor. To which form small beads that refused to mingled with the dirt. Of aversion contracted to small mirror dew globe.Forcing himself to try to back out the soul from this impasse. Instead let the memories of life back home to well. Remembered all the hours on the chair in the dry and sleepy heat of the furnace in the drying house.Something that she even yearned back to. Despite the dull and life-denial environment there, there was still dreams left then. They still unfulfilled fantasies about life over there somewhere. Take me back there, 'she said quietly. They may even imagines, that one should feed the baby down in this hole ...!? It would not surprise me at all, she thought dejectedly. The dog looked up at her with wondering and almost pity eyes. Did not sure why they were still there on the floor. Felt probably just the unmet running in the legs. Would probably just going hunting. Out with the math on new adventures again. Yin patted and stroked its back. Also served as therapy for her. Calming hormones spread namely around in her bloodstream. But it was just then, when she stroked Yang over the back as she knew them. The hard lumps inside dog vest. Obviously knew immediately what it was. Had completely forgotten the dog's vest, and what was there. Zipped up and took out the mobile phone. Stuffed into his hand again and let his fingers enclosing the gun piston. It feels like a gift from the higher powers, she thought. However, never took it up, but concentrated instead on the phone. Saw that the battery life showed half remain and that coverage down there seemed to be nonexistent. Physical quite logical. Down in a police 'cemented and shielding catacombs. Closed, however the phone to cut down power consumption. Before it was stopped back. Thanks to these findings, she felt slightly more satisfied with the situation. The gun was now up on the board and in the game again. Just such a thing. Sometimes felt that it smelled of mold and had to sneeze repeatedly. Although the dog uttered occasionally which probably was sneezing.

Woke up suddenly by something that rattled the grille gate. Had apparently dozed off despite his uncomfortable posture. Thought he saw a woman there in the gloom. Fumbling with his bunch of keys outside the door. Yin was invited, however, only to sit on the floor. All the while the woman put down a tray of food and drink on the floor. Even a bowl of dog food and water just next door. Then locked the door again and the woman disappeared up the stairs. Yin stood at slightly stiff legs. Staggered away from the floor to retrieve träbrickan with today's vital proteins and carbohydrates. Although Yang wagged his tail again. Had certainly felt the smell of food, and even before the Yin even woken up. Had no idea what time it was. But felt so terribly hungry. Just have to have food ... now. Do not care what it tastes, she thought. However, was pleasantly surprised and threw sticks for rapidly spooning into meat stew and rice. What the dog had on her plate, she did not even know. Would probably just lose the appetite of those facts. Only the dog eats sludge hands, so everything is ok. And it seemed the surprisingly well done. Someone caring of the staff had even put there a small chocolate bar. What Yin could not understand why ...!? Maybe the kitchen staff a very different view of humanity than the rest of the police, she assumed. Grateful and slurping she pressed However, in the little sweet, while a further few minutes down the cavity thus could be gilded. Soon discovered that the brain also had their share of energy. Could suddenly think a little more clearly. Felt thus in better balance to logically analyze the resulting situation. Even in such a good shape that she instead began to worry about fingerprints. Yes, those cops had just ripped from her fingers. Could I have left some imprint of that swine, she thought worried. Sure, I had well-gloves on me ... or ?!

After what probably would have been a whole night down there in the icy nest, came a pity soul down with a breakfast tray in his hand. With hot green tea, fried bread and jam of any kind. Announced at the same time Yin, that if an hour or two, she would again. Why, she is no answer. Assumed it was the interrogation would continue. Thanks to the dog's heat, she had made it through the night more or less. However, substantial frozen and trembling cold hands she brought the nice warm cup up to your mouth. Just to hold it was a relief. Feel the warmth spread through his fingers. Then also be defrosted inside of the hot drink is priceless, she thought. The bread with marmalade was also on par with the tea. Tasted like those round the monks who she liked. But now, unfortunately, without it the traditional sugar on the outside. One can not have everything. Especially not like uninvited guest in jail at the police station. While Yang received a bowl of water to his piece of sausage. Or whatever it was for a snack. Yin wondered what the dog really thinking !? Perhaps believe it, that we are sitting here guarding anything. Or you think it nothing at all, and as usual, just living in the moment. Satisfied with little food and few have their pack leader to him.

Just like I said, it took a few hours before a police officer came down and got them. They were brought up to the interrogation room again. Yin, however, again handcuffed with the uncomfortable handcuffs. Had to settle there to await the continuation of the hearing. Yin felt really nothing but experienced mostly a kind of spiritual emptiness. In the hands of anyone other than himself. When the energy is not thinking ahead. A situation without its own control. After a few minutes, came a lone policeman entered the room. Informed her that a parade would be performed. Explained just briefly what would happen. Yin felt the unease take off again. Thought again of fingerprints and its possible consequences. Had she not had the gloves on ... or ...?! Her memory from the time the man was shot was not as clear as it should be. Something sober had obviously remembered more details, she realized with growing uncertainty. Shortly thereafter came another police officer in the interrogation room. Moreover, with a woman walking behind him. Yin perceived her first just as a civilian in colorful clothes. The picture brightened rapidly, however. For when the door is closed and the person stepped forward in its entirety, she saw who it was. Namely Madame Biyu who now stood before her and smiled.

- Well, what do you say? Is Miss woo the woman who you recognize as one of your former employees?
- Miss Woo ... ?? Well, it's all the same she. Yin ... if I remember correctly? She spent some time with me.
- And ... it's you sure?
- Absolutely! No doubt. We were good friends all the time. Did contrast happier at that time. But not so tired and ... excuse me ... worn today.
- The dog is also known as, I understand ...!?
- Aaah dog ... ...? The feeling I also ... of course ...

- Then I ask you ma'am Biyu to follow my colleague to the office during the writing of the guarantor paper and so on.
- Of course!

Both she and a police officer left the room. Madame, however, with a smile on his mouth. An expression that gave Yin a sense of hope. But no more than that. Perceived that not what then would happen. A little surprised that Madame knew the dog. Had never seen it before ...!? It all felt after all slightly confused. She must still admit. At least until the remaining policeman's explanation of the whole situation. Got namely knowing that Madame after a possible identification was willing to pay the bail for her. And, she also would commit to take care of her until the trial. However, according to Madame's own proposal, in exchange for working for her until the bail paid. Yin was also told that she had to go along with the agreement. Instead, she could choose to sit in police custody until trial. The selection was entirely her own. It required, however, no longer time for reflection.Instead became noticeably excited and engaged. Just the thought of to avoid this stinking rat nest can get anyone to agree to almost anything, she said. Although it admittedly was only during the period prior to the trial. A trial ... as she herself put it inside. Now much more confident than just a few hours ago. As yet still down there in källarvalvens obscure and cool catacombs. Without hope for a speedy return to his previous life. How quickly could the real conditions change.

After Madame signed surety papers and pre-paid fee of 10,000 yuan, took the Yin handcuffs. Above all, in order to sign the agreement. She accepted the conditions of the guarantee disclosure. Which was also confirmed by his own signature under the text line ... Miss Yin Woo. The thing was done. Were also given back their personal belongings. Now therefore free to leave the police station. Only with the reservation ... she now instead belonged to Madame Biyu. Both literally and in practice. Something Yin undoubtedly be prepared to accept. Just glad and lucky to have come out from hell. When they leave the station, lacked Madame her purse. Were apparently not left on the floor where she had just put it. Yin sensed something was amiss. Turned and saw Yang away at the end. Wistfully peering out through the glass door. With purse in the jaw. Madame laughed, relieved and thought myself retrieve it. But no! Every time she approached the bag with the hand, the dog growled at her. It ended up that Yin had to pretend to develop some candy from his pocket. Only then let it go.Within minutes they stood, however, all three in the light rain outside the police station. Yin and Yang with Madame at their side. Only now she noticed how dusty her black blazer had become. For it was really not a tidy hotel suite, she spent the night in. In stark contrast to the experience she now instead see the black limousine already screwed. Even with the same driver as last time, she noted. Nodded and smiled shyly recognition to him.Like last time, he opened the doors for them. To be able to comfortably settle in the black gleaming Mercedes. As usual with the same cozy feeling and magical silence when they then slid along the avenue. Away from the gates of hell. In such a car in which only the windshield wiper sweeping motion is the only sound ... and then.

- I thought you never Yin? That we would be seen again in this way ...
- No, not really. I am, as I said really so grateful for this. I do not know ...
- It need not be. You're supposed to, you of course know, work off this debt with me now. To see our agreement out ... right ...!? Cute dog you have, by the way. It was not the last time we met.
- No, I got over it after an uncle who was ill. A friend of mine might say.
- There you go. Life's ways are inscrutable as they say. You never know what tomorrow has in store. It applies to us all. Sometimes it can feel like you won the lottery. In the next second can win ... "slipping through your fingers" ... as they sing the song.
- Well ...

- How lucky for you, I stood at this. Could actually have ignored everything. I mean ... thieves have after all not normally condone, or how.

- No, not usually ...

- But, now, we forget it. We now look forward instead. Against your time with us in our activities.

- Oh, but exactly ... what should I do?

- I'll tell you, when we come to the rest home. First you enjoy a good meal. Can not attend due to other commitments, so to speak.

- M etc .... But ... I think I can not be with you beyond the summer, actually. Should namely feed my child then ... what I know.

- So indeed !? What you know ..!? There you go.

Madame said nothing more on the issue and just took the right towards a sort of driveway. A high gate opened automatically for them. Then the car disappeared down into a garage under the large and impressive villa. Just then Yin suddenly thought of his own apartment. What would she do with it? The rent have to be paid and so on ...!? When they stepped out of the car in the basement garage, she realized, however, that it had become a problem for tomorrow. Namely too much else that is currently occupied her thoughts. Madame, the dog and she left the garage via a lift. After a code opened door. When the elevator stopped and the door opened, they came out into a large hall. Immediately felt a wonderful almost oriental fragrance hit against her. And right next to the elevator was a wide carpeted staircase to the upper floor. Yin was almost dumbfounded by the stylish and solid interior. This is not the home any time, she understood. Madame took them further through a corridor with beautiful modern art on the walls. Until a door also opened with a code. Behind it was a bright and cheerful room. With bed, armchair and some other matching furniture. She explained to Yin, the room usually was for their guests. However, even she and the dog at the moment could keep there. Both toilet and shower were additionally adjacent to the room. Was again informed that the food would shortly be served in the room, as I said. She wanted something, there was a button to call for staff at. Yin was familiar with all the practical details, when Madame eventually left the room. Struck instinctively TV 's and threw himself on the bed. Felt totally exhausted by the time the police station. Both physically and mentally. Yang was however on the floor for once.Was not quite the same. Yin had almost fallen asleep when a woman dressed in black with a white apron entered the room. With him she had a tray of food and drink. Said little, but just nodded and disappeared again.Perhaps the most to Yang growled at her ...?! Yin just took advantage. Serve the food in the room, who can complain, she thought ...!? The mere sight of fragrant food made her fully aware of how hungry she was. It did not take long for her to put in the whole chicken stew with peanuts and rice. A little strange, however, that just beer served with the meal, she thought. But considered that it actually fit perfectly. Bitterness in beer harmonized namely with the slightly more sweet and sour stew in a pleasurable way. The dog got exactly the same right in a bowl separately. Besides beer, of course. Despite it saw more than pleased. After the meal, she sank down on the bed again. Measured, but somehow still completely blank in the head. Maybe it was all of the impressions in the last day which overloaded her psyche. Now could not the brain to take in more simply.

Eventually she woke calm and pleasant background sound from the TV 's. Along with the dog snoring. Was most surprised that she did not wake up in the basement of the police station. So strong was namely Stay characterized her. Instead, she could now just breathe out and really enjoy the wide soft bed. By chance she cast a glance toward the door. Discovered that it had no doorknobs. So nothing that you could open it with ...!? Just a code lock and a small fixed handle. At least turn to the toilet are on this side of the door, she had time to just think. Before the more unpleasant realization hit her. I'm actually locked up in this room, she realized, and stood up out of bed. Went to the door and checked. No, there was no way to get out of. Without code words. Strange ...!? Pondering for a while, but ac-

cepting it as a present fact. Sat down, however slightly
more miserable in the armchair. Moved instead look to
the television screen. There appeared some kind of
Chinese soap. For lack of a better ... she thought, and
confirmed their indifference to increasingly ignore. Behind the eyelids, she could not completely stifle
the thought of the locked door. It bothered her inner
peace somehow. Uncertainty had unexpectedly returned
seeped into. What was it that was not true? Even Yang
stood below her on the floor almost glared. Wondered
the sensed or the no. Yes, it did.

Two long and dreary days had already passed and Yin
was still in his room. All the time with the same routine
when it came the food and drink. Always at specified
times strangely. While coffee was served and then. Some
of the staff had even asked if she smoked. Although this
was denied. To just after almost wish that she had
done. A cigarette that at least pass the time. Had even
dared to question the lady who served the food, so the
door could not be opened from the inside. The answer
to Yin was that it is a safety issue. With that information
she received settle. However, tried to peek when the lady on the road knocked out in the code, but could unfortunately not perceive it. An hour later in the evening,
a man came up to her. A brawny guy with bare
head. No she seen before. After all, quite properly

dressed in a dark suit. However, equipped with an ugly and incomprehensible tattoo on his neck. Although Yang yelled angrily, he stood unprovoked straddled with his arms crossed, and said ...

- You can get ready now. About one hour, you are transported further down to Hong Kong.
- Hong Kong ..?! What should I do there?
- What to do there. If you have not taken it ... or ...?
- Glance !? There seems to be a lot that you should adopt on this place. Answer me this question instead!
- If now no one has explained it to you, so ... you should to Mongkok Paradise. One of the finer whorehouses in the neighborhood.
- And ... what should someone like me doing in a whorehouse if so ..? Cleaning might ...
- Ha ha ha ... well, it was good. Clean !? Yes, in a way. You will in any case get a taste of broom handle ... ha ha ha .... But, as I said ... get ready now. We will soon get you.
- I am also pregnant! So there.
- Surely ...!? If nothing else, perhaps you can become it. Ha ... ha ... ha ...

Suddenly it dawned on Yin, what all this was. She would then pay off their debt in a whorehouse. In Mongkok Paradise !? Probably one of all Madame's "great places" in which the company, you could guess. Well, it's that

she support themselves and their menagerie, now realized Yin. Therefore, such a nice house with its own staff
and chauffeur. Nice cars and luxury living. And now
they had caught a rat to the cage. How friendly can a
man play and still be a real pig under the surface? It was
something that amazed her, while she paced back and
forth in the room. Madame ...!? Yes, indeed. It should
perhaps have suspected !? But, now I know anyway, she
noted with a sigh. She is thus a real bitch, the
whore. Yin alternated between sitting in bed and that as
a troubled spirit floating around between the
walls. Plans began to be eventually structured. Shaped to
a chess game in her brain. It was important to think of
several moves in advance. And even alternative coun-
termove course. The goal must of course be, to get the
black lady checkmate. Although the white pieces right
now was at a disadvantage. More incredible collections
have certainly occurred throughout history, she believed. And ... why not expand the historic chess history
with another such party ...?

Wondered desperately up until the door an hour later
opened. It was the bald man who now also had with
him a colleague. A smaller type with more Mongolian
appearance. However, just as muscular and with the
same tough attitude. The strange thing was, however,
that both bar nyputsade and shiny black shoes, she
thought. Did not quite understand why they needed

it. In that particular industry as they apparently worked in other words ...?! How right she had other things to think of. Was immediately asked to bring their things and follow them out of the room. A man in front of her and one behind. Yang, she luckily lead yourself through the corridor. Until the elevator that once took them down to the basement garage. Now, however, to another car. A kind of SUV with large wheels. Even so high, that Yin almost got the feeling of having to climb into the car. Once in the back seat, she noted, that the windows were dark and just barely translucent. Is it perhaps too ... "a safety issue," she asked sarcastically. With the men in the front seat pulled the set off with screeching tires of the painted concrete floor. Up from the garage and down against the steel gate. The as well as on the command willingly opened slowly. While waiting for it, they said to her, that she from now got to shut up. I, hitherto button saying a word, she thought with hatred growing within him. The men, however, slowed down the tempo during the continuation of the journey through the city. Darkness had several hours settled over Guangzhou. To re-awaken neon lights, lamps and colored signs. Normally, the number of streetlights in Chinese cities say the least in the minority. Especially in smaller towns and villages. Usually even non-existent. The men chatting quietly with each other.Most of Yin could not hear. Was still not interested in their conversation but thought most of his own plan. However, increasingly unsure how realistic its implementation was indeed. Did understood that if the plan were to succeed, it must be executed before Guangzhou city limit had passed. Otherwise, it would lead to other more geographical and logistical problems, so to speak. She followed the traffic all the time through the unstained windshield and was only waiting for the right moment. Had already provided both himself and Yang preventive protective equipment. That is some old cotton balls which thankfully remained in his jacket breast pocket. Now compact pressed in both their ear canals. Had also taken up the gun from the dog's vest. The weapon that was now armed and ready in her slightly trembling hand. The dog, however lay completely still and unconcerned down on the floor. Safe unaware of what would soon happen.

Blood on their hands

They had just passed through a suburb with dark narrow streets and just stopped in the left lane at a red light. Probably in waiting to swing out to the larger highway S303 south. It could go a few seconds before the Yin overcame his indecision. Turned his head to make sure that no car was behind them. No there yet anyway, she noted with increased confidence. Felt almost as digitally programmed for the task. Also dealt literally under that program. The shot rang out with a terrible roar. To be followed by another. This also equally deafening. Yang rotated howling around down there on the floor, while a gunpowder-smelling smog filled the cabin. Both the bright car roof and her face was immediately rödprickiga of blood that momentarily showered the immediate surroundings. The heavy recoil from the weapon are literally struck her arm straight up to the ceiling in both shots. It felt more like luck, the gun is not pulled away from her frail little hand. Was certainly not experienced and accurate marksman. Although as they say, practice makes perfect. However, had the rare mental cooling required. Is in fact not many people manage to so relatively callous eliminate two human lives in this manner. For the eliminated was no exaggeration to call them. The two muscle bikers in the front seat who sat motionless and bent forward with his head down between his legs. Both, each with a red hole in the back of the head and undoubtedly stone dead. Without analyzing the situation upholstered Yin quickly down the weapon in his jacket pocket. While she burned easily in the hot barrel. Without either know or take notice of it. For now there was only one thing that loomed. As quickly as possible to get out of the car. However, as was the portion of the plan is not entirely according to the drawings. Tore desperately at the rear door handles and locks, but nothing happened. The car hummed still unconcerned idling. But the doors did not open. The seconds passed and the traffic lights turned green. Took not long until a car behind them honked. Felt panic come. Which did not become less of a dog howling and barking down on the floor. Finally realized that there was only one thing to do. Namely, to try to get out through the front doors. Therefore, began to squeeze through the narrow space between the front seats. With some effort, she succeeded with it. Then it was just crawling over the corpse in the passenger seat and try to open the door. For the dog, who instinctively followed his mistress, went more easily understood. When the car behind them honked for the second time, Yin finally got up the front door and Yang was fast first man out. Afraid and shocked as it was. It rang still in her ears after gun shots, when the two went back to the street direction. Past the car that had just tutat on them. There they had already vevat down the window and looked aghast at her. In contrast white and ghostly light from another car that also forced to stop behind the first. The ghost they saw, was a young and pale girl with bloodstains on both the face and hands. Moreover, with polka dots and patches of reddish brown hair. Her bright chinos were also two-toned. Now in red and beige as the result of climbing over the bloody passenger. She shouted at them in the car, they had been shot and that she now has to call the police. Then she went on and the dog running backwards along the hard shoulder. To eventually take off onto a smaller darkened side street and quickly disappear from sight. As far as possible from all the curious who in increasing numbers began to gather around "the shot at the car."

For a long time she stood hunched and panting inside an unlit backyard. Out of breath and exhausted after stepping march. Probably no idea how hideous she looked. Bloodstains and red splashes everywhere on the body.Could actually have frightened the life out of the toughest in there in the dark alley. Unaware of this fact, she went blithely into an adjacent restaurant and asked to borrow the toilet. They wondered understood to mean, in all its day she had done ..!? They got some incoherent explanation for answers. Something about ... that she had slaughtered two pigs. With the incomprehensible reason they let her after all borrow it. It was not, but that she herself was shocked by the sight of his own creation in the bathroom mirror. So she looked !? Even Yang looked stunned at her. Self had escaped with only a few small drops of blood on the coat. In addition to its red paws of course. Truly a friend in need ... Yang, she thought. While she gratefully found a bottle with liquid soap above the washbasin. Smudged carefully the cream into the face and hair. Then with cupped hands rag with water. Held securely in the ten minutes before the mirror image considered themselves satisfied. Then attempted to ruffle the hair dry. Which just went ... so there. Was at least glad the color of the jacket. On the black fabric synthesis does not bloodstains to the same extent. The bright trousers, however, nothing to do about it, she realized. At least not right now and here. With still wet mop, she left the toilet and thanked one of the waiters for the loan. Then ordered a glass of orange liqueur. Out of habit, you could say. Must quickly get into something that can calm nerves, she felt. Swept glass with a half time. Then settled into a soft plush sofa and sipped the rest. The dog was given a bowl of water. Indeed, without her even asked about it ...!? After half an hour, she asked them to call a cab. Did not even think that she herself had a private phone in dog vest. In addition, right next to the gun which also had just regained their ordinary place. After a careful and thorough cleaning with soap and water.

In the taxi, she closed her eyes all the way home. Wanted to shield themselves from reality and all the impressions from outside. Felt upset inside. Not without reason, of course. The next few days had shaken her hard. And even got her to think about. The result of an unusual and self-critical analysis. An awakening where she from now felt compelled to choose a less risk-averse route than before. Have simply gone beyond the limits of my own boldness, she realized. In almost felt as invulnerable. As also obviously penalized itself. Only close to for a long time stuck in the Chinese legal machinery. However, could not deny that Madame Biyu same time was the person who actually become her rescue. Despite the hatred that she now felt toward her. Madam with large B. Wondering just how big her empire really is, she thought. Probably more than anyone can imagine. Yin final plane comprised namely that she would in any way to tell if Madame police operations. But felt no longer so sure. Had namely listed in the station that the police officer there had been an extra bankroll of her. Banknotes which he quickly stuffed into their own pockets. Something fishy was in the relationship between the police and her. She bribed his way was not a bold guess, considered Yin. Stood therefore now in two minds between the two options. Should she or should not she. Still brooding over the issue when the taxi pulled up outside her home. Finally at home again, she sighed. Step relieved of the car and gave the astonished driver a generous tip.Then let Yang doing their needs in the darkness inside the bushes, before they both enthusiastically hurried toward the entrance. Yang completely pulled her up the whole staircase. Was probably so happy and excited to finally come home again. The door opened and shut. Yin could hardly believe it, but now they were truly home again. The room with the normally trapped and slightly stale air felt despite it being pure paradise to return to.Danced around on the floor a few laps in a ritual of gratitude, where even the dog went on his way. Before the two with a leap took the bed in a horizontal position. Never had she appreciated his own bed as much as now.Especially for these risky and unpredictable adventure on the slack rope. Days which should be rapidly forgotten. Especially for his mental well-being ahead. That she understood.

The bloody pants were thrown in a heap beneath the bed. Any other signs of past drama synthesis, however. The evening was late and they both had then an hour back stamped out for the day. The light was extinguished, and the only sound was their snuff from the bed. Where they now lay close together. Rocked the SOMS of the last days bewildering intricacies and improbable events. Despite the worst possible odds were Yin then return back. But for how long ... yes, it knew of course not. Probably also already called in the whole Guangzhou.

A few days later they had still not left the apartment. Apart from Yang's regular and needs-consuming breaks in the backyard. Admittedly, throughout southern China since a couple of days back besieged by a rain filled low pressure, but it was not the whole explanation. Rather, it was self-preservation that kept her at home. Did ... or at least assumed she was now a hunted quarry. With blood on their hands additionally. And as such, it felt too risky to unnecessarily expose themselves out on the city streets and squares. Better to lie low for a while than to tempt fate again. During these days of soul-searching and reflection crystallized out of necessity, revised self-image. Realizing the fact that she could no longer continue as before. Had already had a taste of the bitter consequences of his opportunist and chance-taking life. Consequences that also all too easily escalate to unimagined consequences. Also felt a budding homesickness within. A spiritual vacuum which is just waiting to be filled. And there really was no other way to fulfill it, than to go home. Greet their dear ones at home. Although it also felt a bit like a defeat. Being forced to surrender. Openly having to show their vulnerability and loss of independence. Exposing his own crumbling pride. Such always feels heavy and degrading. But the alternatives were probably even worse. After all, it's only a temporary visit, consoled herself with. Get some new energy and joy of life and then reunited with the city again. So it was all planned. With the intention contradicted journey home with confidence and desire. Would only just be sure to get that necklace sold. So that really was "in funds", so to speak. Do not come home from a failed pauper.

A brother without mother

On Tuesday morning, February 4, she stood in the check-in queue at the airport. For the day wearing his black fur jacket. During which she wore a white polo shirt with gray melange pants and half-high black shoes. Beside her stood a red suitcase. With excessive amounts of dog hair on. Both here and there. The culprit was standing next to. Now without a dog vest wearing. Or rather ... low. Yang yawned constantly. Probably as an expression of boredom, one can guess. And Yin felt the same thing. Gender creeps too slowly forward, she thought. Today we're going out and fly you and I, she said, patting both the dog and its nascent small stomach. Whoever still not showed any major signs, what the summer would are coming. As hand luggage, she had a black backpack with red stripes on. There, inside the low-including all of the money from the recently sold the necklace.Specifically, 95,000 yuan in cash notes. Tightly wrapped in protective plastic. It was certainly less than the original valuation. But felt nonetheless fully satisfied. So much money she had never seen at one time before. Felt as a nouveau riche home comers. And both rich and on the way home was just what she was. Would soon board the plane to Hengyang. A relatively short flights and much faster and smoother than the train. Had also planned to open an account and deposit the money in a bank there in Hengyang. While a debit card would be attached to the account. Thought namely become more civilized from now.

It was on a Boeing 737 from the Hainan Airlines, which she then boarded. A completely new factory plan pointed out the flight attendant who welcomed them aboard the flight to Hengyang. Yin had a window seat well ahead of the plane and began to feel some anxiety inside. Not the least of the problem with the seat belt. Had namely never flown before. Just such a thing. Though what most occupied her attention was all the same backpack. The she released either time or gaze away. There was the whole of her future stored. It was in any case so, she thought. When during the steep climb left Guangzhou behind. The city is now slowly vanished in a gray haze of haze and smog. All while wind noise at the same rate rose in the cabin. Felt both arousal and fear at the same time. But mostly it was a fantastic feeling. To fly for the first time. What if the mother could see me now, it hit her. Just when the plane made a turn and sun rays broke through the window. And my brother ... and the old classmates ...!? Wondering what everyone would think ... if only they knew? Recumbent only she enjoyed the view down over the clouds. Really felt that they were flying. However, it was not long until the engine speed began to drop. The approach to Hengyang has already begun, she thought. My, how fast it went !?The sign for "seat belt on" lit up in the ceiling. The call she could be ignore. Had not even been able to take of it. When they eventually returned sank down through the clouds, she thought with some disappointment, that they would have been allowed to continue for one hour. So exciting and wonderful it was.

Stepped into the first best taxi and went directly to the Bank. One place in Hengyang known. Had the fact been there with his mother a few times. After the account is opened and the money placed there, she got after some wait even its new Visa debit card in your hand. Gold colored additionally! Felt almost like a grown woman, when she walked out of the bank. The fur jacket with sunglasses on. Stopped where a new taxi on the street. What was ordered directly to the home. The old farm in the middle of tobaksfältens womb. Her own original home. Was so excited that she could not sit still. Now, after all, not because of the worn and rough leather couch in the back seat. Without leaning forward and just focused on the way home. When there were only a few kilometers left, came a cyclist straight toward them on the narrow road. It was a woman with a shawl around her head.They had to slow down considerably. Everything that she would not have to run down into the ditch. The moment they passed each other, got Yin a strange feeling that it was her mother. Immediately turned on. However, most to convince himself that she was mistaken. But wherever she looked, she could no longer see the woman. Maybe she had fallen into the ditch anyway. Or maybe disappeared into any path or you ...?! Yin could not think more about it. The driver asked with some hesitation in his voice, if they were really on the right path. Just laughed in response and assured him of his good sense of the place. Had namely cycled there countless times before. Recognize each small trees and large stones along the way. It had even been her cycling route to school for many years. Soon it was just the long hill left up to the house. Felt the rising pulse pounded in his head.What will they say now that they suddenly get to see me again, she asked almost in tears. When the taxi stopped in front of the house, seemed not a man to the outside in the courtyard. The driver loaded from her luggage.The generous gratuity she gave, was quite on a par with the bank account and her great happiness to be home again. A few bucks that also noticeably brightened the taxi driver's day. The familiar sound of cackling ducks still felt like a välkomstkör for her.

Only when the taxi disappeared behind her, she discovered, that not everything was as before at home. Did not understand what it was. Was long left with the suitcase and looked wonderingly about him. Until it suddenly dawned on her. Where had the drying house gone somewhere ...?! Well, just where it had stood, there was now only dark and sooty stones from the foundation remains. What on earth could have happened to it, she thought with growing concern. While an unknown woman came out the front door. Disappeared, however, just as quickly back in again. Yin wondered, of course, who it could be. Could at least see that it was not her mother.Stepfather appeared not to. Only someone who suddenly loomed to one of the windows. To seconds after discovering his little brother. Come running out down the stairs toward her. Calling her name all the way. Until they threw themselves into each other's arms. Yang barked excitedly while both sisters cried. At best, they could snuffle out each other's names. Actually, without saying so much more. Yin realized how much he missed her. And also how much she longed for him. All the emotions welled up inside her. Clearly had too long been repressed. He looked astonished up and down on her. On her hair and the new hairdo. On the nice clothes that also smelled so good of her perfume. Stood a long time, and only felt on the fine fur jacket. Almost as if he never wanted to stop. However, it seemed to force a else that he wanted to get out of it. Something choked themselves. Yin understood and wondered how it was with him. What is it that you want to say Zhinsun, she asked comforting?

- Mom ...
- What? Mom?
- Well ... mom ... mom is dead.
- Mom !? It can not be possible ...!? I met the ...
- Joo, actually ... she is there. Mom ...
- Death ?! Mom? Not well, she ... I've gifts with me to her ...
- Long believed that you were also dead. We were so sad ... all the time ... indeed.
- Poor thing! But ... do not cry. I have gifts for you ... well.

Yin sat down on the ground. The legs carried her no longer. Yang stood by and licked her tears ceaselessly running down your face. Instinctively understood that she needed comfort. All the while his brother now increasingly became aware that she had a dog with them.

- It's called Yang and it is my best friend.
- Yang ...!?
- Yeah. Sit here with me and tell me. You need not be afraid anymore. I'm here with you now. Do you understand?
- Mmmm ...!?
- I have been in Guangzhou constantly. It knows you, where it is !? I know right? You enjoyed my gift? The car ...!?
- Mmmm ...

- Yeah, but now tell me. What happened ?!

Despite all tried Yin to collect himself. Big sister as she was. Held him tight and comforting to him. Where they now sat all three in the middle of the court-yard. Complied by the woman whose face could be glimpsed at the kitchen window. Curious and obviously wondering Yin's sudden return. Zhinsun sniffled a few times. Scratched the dog of the neck and then began slowly to tell ...

It was an incredible and shocking story that she had to take part of. After what she knew, had stepfather's infidelity business to take, then Yin left the farm. Often he was gone all weekend. Apparently, even angry and intimidating at night when he came home after their adventures. The mother and he argued for the most part in connection with these incidents. On the whole atmosphere had not been the best for the rest either. He had also accused her of having thrown away the gun. Accused her also to have been instrumental to Yin's sudden disappearance. Assumed they were in cahoots with each other. According to the boy, the mother had taken all this very hard, and apparently often been miserable and sad. Zhinsun had during a bike ride in the distance seen heavy black smoke rising from the farm. Whether there really was something that burned was still uncertain. After stepping completely out of the cycle, he could well back home only conclude that the drying house burned. Or rather ... almost already burned down. It smelled tobacco smoke throughout. Had cried out loud without getting any response. Looked everywhere but not a human in sight. Rode therefore urgently to the nearest neighbor to ask for help. They in turn alerted the fire brigade. Once received it, however, most focus on, to isolate the fire from the other buildings. The drying house and all the tobacco that existed there, there was mostly just carbon and ash remain. Yin's stepfather had also found somewhere. Also came on the bike eventually. Drunk swerved into the courtyard. Then went mostly just around and swore ... that Zhinsun put it.

Because the mother was missing, feared that she had been left in the dryer housing. A growing number of neighbors gathered at the farm. Most of the slaking but of course also as a consolation for the family. That is ... for Zhinsun first. Stepfather got his solace in the even more liquor. Something thus made him even less popular in the countryside. Than he already was. Only after a few hours of fighting was one of the neighbors that horrible discovery. Had gone into standby shed to look for a shovel, when he saw her. The mother then! Hanging down a rope from a wooden beam in the ceiling. Obviously taken off himself. All were obviously distressed and upset. Except stepfather still just swore and blamed everything on the ... hell. And to some extent also the mother herself. The police were called immediately and on a first examination, they found a letter under her sweater.There was the whole explanation written down. And the drying house, she had set itself on fire. At least it was exactly what she was supposed to do. According to the intentions of the letter. As a pure revenge against their so-called ... husband. For all he has done to her and the family. According to what she wrote, also for causing Yin's escape from the farm. For his boozing and above all for his infidelity with ... "that bitch to the woman," as it were. Also for its increasingly less interest in the estate and responsible for operations there. Simply had not managed anymore. Saw no end to the misery. While she was in the letter asked his two children to apologize. She loved them more than anything else at this hell planet, as she finished the letter.

Yin sat long on the couch in the kitchen and read the mother's heartfelt letter. What Zhinsun hidden behind a painting in his room. All to no stepfather and his new woman would destroy it. Only now he dared to produce it.To his confidential own sister. The only living who still went to rely on. The words of the letter felt Yin mother's own voice that spoke to her. The tears from her disconsolate but still crying turned the hand-written words to a blurry glow in his eyes. A poignant testament so naked brokered the mother's last wishes and thoughts. Futility lay heavily over the kitchen, where she sat with Yang and brother at his side. The future seemed suddenly foiled. Felt almost devastated and completely empty inside. The man she loved most in life no longer existed. How can you stand it, she wondered Supplied? Just do not understand how ...? The thought of her mother's gift which still remained in the suitcase was too unbearable. To not get to experience the joy that she probably would have given expression. Especially considering with the care and love Yin had selected it. The pain of this incomprehensible fact tormented throughout her wounded and despairing soul. Whatever she was going to do for her mother to come would be completely in vain. The idea was unimaginable. Ironically, when the economic opportunities now finally existed. Not even when she got the opportunity to thank and pamper her. Their own single mother. Suddenly thought also of the small child who then would come. Not even that she would get to experience. Becoming a grandmother that is. Understood, however, and also saw that Zhinsun experienced the same despair of their situation. The responsibility for him fell the now her lot. For he must surely be taken care of by someone. And who ... except she herself could it ?! He could not be left in that pack. In stepfather and his magpie to the mistress. It felt totally out of the question! Especially considering what she's already seen the constellation. What would become of growing up with such examples? A boozer without impulse control, and a chain-smoking hookers. Well, the woman actually looked as such. Right now, for example. When she stood in the doorway and stared at them. Gum-chewing with casually crossed legs and a smoking cigarette in hand. Dressed in low-cut dirty blouse, short leather skirt and fishnet stockings. No thanks, no such stepmom is not my brother deserved, she thought of defying gaze toward the creature in the room. However, she would have fit well on the Paradise where Mongkok in Hong Kong. Actually had not even had to change clothes!

The moments when the stepfather was home, he sat mostly in front of the TV 's with his legs on the table and drank beer. With the ever blazing the slut next door. When Yin cooked some food or some time accidentally happened to be within earshot of him, overwhelmed, she quips. The drying house and her mother's suicide was her fault. Even the farm's incipient decline could be attributed to her. The only one without guilt was obviously his. Whose statements also as a parrot often repeated by his appendage of woman. Not even Yang felt any sympathy for them. Growled rather often when they came near him. Yin did not so much. Knew that she and Zhinsuns stay there soon would be just a memory. Also had prepared him for, how their resignation from the farm would go to. And even when and where they then thought go. He was both happy and excited. Fully understand the plans for their definitive departure from the yard. To also get to accompany his sister out into the world felt like a realized adventure novel for him.

One afternoon a few days later Zhinsun cycling at full speed. Easy sweaty after the ride home from school. As soon Yin saw him skidding into the courtyard, she took up her phone. Called as predetermined and agreed upon by a taxi. Stepfather was not at home and the woman was his best in showering. Would apparently keep to where in the bathroom some afternoons. And this was apparently one of them. However, it took against Yin, that whatsoever imagine, that appendage sitting in her own mother's old bathtub and Loga itself. Namely, in the same bathtub where the mother often in the evenings drawing off the hot water. A spa resort with twenty medical herbs. Was upset by the thought. But for now it fits well that she is there, thought Yin already packed everything. Both her brother and her bags were already ready to go below the front steps. Everything was ready. Just waiting car. The taxi would soon take them to the Hengyang Airport. She laughed, relieved and hugged Zhinsun. Saw the delight in his eyes. Yes, the whole he was beaming with happiness. Finally, he would be free from the wretched life that fate so unfair given him. School friends he would indeed miss, but there was no explicit troubled him. Significantly, however, his incessant curiosity, if not the taxi would soon come. Could not really believe in it all, until they actually sat there in the car. Towards aviation. However, there were no flights booked. Without Yin hoping for a couple of vacancies at some time during the evening. Otherwise, they were well sleep over in the departure hall ...!? Worse things could endure. The car took a while. Even so, they waited patiently. Until the engine noise suddenly heard. Almost at the same time they saw a taxi pop up over the hill. More awaited than ever. They literally threw the bags and themselves in the car. And Yang of course, was first in. Liked to travel by car. Shortly thereafter appeared only a cloud of dust behind them. Indeed, the only concrete that briefly testified about their hasty departure from the yard. They turned around several times down the hill, but no one seemed to have seen them. Unnoticed, they could finally leave his disrupted childhood home behind. On the way to the airport for onward transport to Guangzhou. Of Yin's own experience with the only certainty ... that the future ... by its nature is usually characterized by very ... uncertainty.

The time was 21:40, when the "fasten seatbelt" sign re-ignited. They had begun to descend towards Guangzhou. Zhinsun almost since inception sat with his nose against the cabin window, was now forced to Yin's re-

quest to put to the right and take the belt. The adventure for his part had just begun. The flight itself was a dream suddenly come true. Amazement he followed everything that happened both in the cabin and outside. The two often looked at each other and smiled contentedly. Realizing that they would soon be "at home". Beyond the reach of his former guardian. Or whatever you would call them? Packet, was perhaps the most adequate name !? What Yin also increasingly begun to use. For Zhinsuns cheer estimate additionally.
- Zhinsun! You will soon become the uncle.
- What? Who ..?
- Well you! You ... will become uncle, I said. Because I have a little baby in the belly.
- Have you .. ??
- Yeah ..! Are not you glad? A little toddler to care for and play with ...
- Mmm ...

He smiled the most. Looked surprised and thoughtfully into her eyes. A baby? His own sister ...? Could not really take in the whole thing. With a wicked smile, he looked back out the window. Towards the ground now came closer and closer and finally with a thud received flight HA 338 from Hengyang.

Revenge is sweet

They heralded joint first days in Guangzhou was devoted mostly to practical things. As to arrange a school for Zhinsun. Which, however, was not easy. You need an attestation from the old school. In addition, even more control talks with the errant stepfather. After a lot of ifs and buts superiors, however, everything. The brother was even quartered at a local school just a few blocks away. She was also forced to purchase a mattress for him.Instead of now having to sleep in her bed. Most things, in addition to the mattress, could now be purchased on her new debit card. Felt so simple and practical, she thought. For so long she had it financially very well off. At least by her standards. The account is filled to the brim ... as she herself put it. Pondered despite that even submit her second necklace for auction firm. Might as well spooned out while the soup is hot ... as the saying solder.One evening, when they came home from the plaza in town, got the Yin one idea. While Zhinsun lay on her mattress along with Yang and slöläste some comic books, she began to make new plans. The goal of her uppblommade creativity this time namely himself Madame Biyu. So easy, she should not escape, thought Yin. The method for her revenge emerged increasingly during the evening. The music from the radio as Zhinsun listened to, somehow became a kind of inspiration for her thoughts and ideas. In contrast to many other figured she usually better to music. Among other things, why the radio was for the most part on. Dog vest, who since leaving the childhood home hung in the small hall, caught now her interest. Or rather, it was the gun that lay inside. Zhinsun looked wide-eyed, as she entered the room. Because he thought he recognized it as the stepfather, he assumed, too, that the recently been stolen from him. As also admitted by his direct request. Revealed however that the already low in the suitcase, the time she left the family and the farm. Thought not tell him about the improbable events that have taken place in relation to the weapon itself. Nor about the people who had caused it all. All this horrible she hid deep in his innermost corner.

When the light was extinguished that night, the plan was more or less finished. Only some practical details remained to realize the sweet revenge. She looked forward to it. Although she probably did not himself had become spectators to vend engage first climax. It would be too risky, she said. Especially in view of its own history concerning Madame Biyu and her running dogs morbid fate. On the contrary, she should lie low, when it came to its own public exposure. Maybe it was not just the police who were after her. It was easy to figure out. They play does not go unpunished with these mafia-like company. However, what worried her most was that she certainly was sought after. Maybe that as "the young Chinese lady with her dog." What malfunctioned to her life in a limiting manner. Before she became significantly easier identifiable by having the dog with him. A fact that seriously occupied her thoughts. One solution would be to Yang always walked connected in Zhinsuns hand. And ... they did go a little for themselves before her. Applied only to give an adequate explanation for his brother. Could not tell the real truth. The solution to the problem was simply that Zhinsun would take over responsibility for the dog's upbringing forward. And that therefore she would walk a few steps before or after them.Something that really sounded illogical and silly. However, something must surely be done ... until further notice. If they dare to show themselves out then. In some cases, they could of course leave the dog at the cafe Chawan or the girls at the factory.

I will namely send a small gift for a lady that I know. That was the explanation that Zhinsun did when he and Yin arrived at the small post office. Asked him to wait outside with Yang. He who had just come home from school and wanted to go with out a turn. In the morning, she had carefully washed the so-called "gift". Then soaked in expensive perfume addition. Thought namely booze in it would wipe all fingerprints. Even the few cartridges that were left were cleaned. Dried since the gun with a freshly washed towel, before it was closed in a box. With an attached note on which was written ' *Save it as a memory. Thank you for your* cooperation! "The package she wrote the name and the address at which stood at Madame Biyus old business cards. All this was done with the gloves on. Never has a gun ever smelled so good, she thought with an inner smile. With the smile lingering she left the post office. With Zhinsun and the dog a few steps ahead of him. Yang was a bit puzzled. Had not yet become accustomed to the new "security routine" and often turned his head to check the mistress presence in the flock. Eventually, they slipped into their local tribal cafe. Because ... as Yin thought ... celebrate the first step on the refined revenge. The exquisite plan that is not a living soul knew. Hopefully, however, more when it came to its future consequences. Each with a donut and Coca-Cola enjoyed most of time together there at the window. In the new reality that the fate of the present, assisted them. Not least Yin knew that continue had to live in the present. And the best way to manage the life they both so drastically forced to reboot. Zhinsun then started again wonder, who was the father of that baby in her growing belly. But Yin just smiled at him and said, that the tale I'll tell you another time.

After a ten-day long wait, she executed the second and final part of the plan. It was namely the time during which the packet should have reached the receiver. That is, Madame Biyu. And ... even if she occasionally been on a short trip "in service", she should now have received the gift in his hand. In other words, hopefully, also left their fingerprints on it. To ensure that the last part of the plan would succeed, she multiplade it. When some adequate address information was found, sent three identical letters to as many recipients. With the same textual content. They were issued to the judicial police in Guangzhou, the head of the Homicide Squad and the local police office, where Madame Biyu lived. Yin wrote in broken Chinese ...

" *It thins the murder of the two Madame Biyu employed men dead in the black car at gatkorsning Tuhua Rd. and 303-ball, South China Express <u>and</u> another murder of the man Luohan chean. He lives* at the hardware store *Li W ŭ j in N Sh A ngdi à np on Kengkou Rd Street. You b o rg island ra a unders island felt at home at* Madame Biyu *the address Hongfu 1 pc. Street (Tuhucun) for murder gun safe there with her.* I am anonymous witness. *Would tell you that I actually* know *precisely* she is the murderer . *For both of them. Check ball grooves in the gun barrels. Actually belonged to Find murder pistols so. And fingerprints !! She has many whorehouses. For example Mongkok Paradise in Hong Kong* "

The day after the letter was sent commenced a new daily routine. Every morning when Zhinsun was in school, she and the dog namely a taxi bound for Madame Biyu. Or rather, so she asked the driver to drive to a petrol station which was right next door. Had previously vigilant noted the station through the car window. Namely, during the evening when the two now meritorious dead men forced her into the car from the villa. Every day that passed the taxi home, she controlled the situation there. Both outside and inside the gates. However, on the third day, she received a pacifier, you might say. Then the whole place was occupied by police cars and the gate was open. Even some police officers could see inside and outside the cars. Yin asked the driver to drive slowly past. Pretended to be sure of the destination address. But of course, just to enjoy the situation as long as possible. Although I may never find out, how life ends for this ... Madame Biyu, she thought. Considered despite the Revenge had succeeded. "Mission completed" ... as you put it in the film world! Yin from Gouzishan is actually no one unpunished lurking, she thought proudly, and gave Yang. All the while the taxi soon ordered against China Plaza. This would be celebrated!

However, as was held the first real party next weekend. Then she invited out all the girls from the factory. Long since returned from their New Year celebrations. However, without telling the real reason for the party. It was obviously too incredible and cruel to ever be reproduced. Therefore, she slipped on the truth firmly and fantasized together a suitable credible reason. On Saturday evening we all gathered at Xinxinshan. An upscale restaurant on Beijing Road. Only after taking a unifying walk around the small lake in the park at the Martyrs' Cemetery. A peaceful and relaxing oasis in the otherwise uninspiring surroundings. Zhinsun felt really omsvärmad and looked after by all the girls. Especially after they took part of the mother's fate. It was so tragic it all. Yet, Yin for the first time since sadness bid finally smile relaxed and breathe out. After all unlikely that happened to her recently. Felt nevertheless happy throughout the evening. Really enjoyed all the food and drink. To not talk about being together with their friends. More than grateful she realized that this nice restaurant of the moment instead could have been a completely different place. A nasty place, even. If not fate so friendly and haphazard stretched out its helping hand at the right time. She even appreciated when one of the girls at a time, gently stroking her stomach and wondered how the little one was doing ...?! Received a warm smile back. Seemed almost resigned to their fate. For the evening she wore a change a completely newly purchased necklace with a silver dragon in the pendant. A Dragon ... as in China namely symbolize ... strength. And right strength ... is something that really characterizes Yin. Anything else would be unfair to say.

One rainy afternoon over a month after the friends pleasant gathering at Xinxinshan could again see Yin with slightly rounded belly roam inside the eastern railway station's Great Hall. Now also with his brother Zhinsun.Seemingly calm and relaxed in the crowding of all stressed travelers. Not least because she had just bought her own apartment for almost all the money that yet another sold-diamond necklace had yielded. A modern and bright two-room apartment on the sixth floor with wonderful views of the Pearl River. Not yet furnished with nothing but two beds, a table and some chairs. Plus some colorful expressionist paintings hastily procured from a gallery in the same block. Zhinsun had also been forced to change schools. Which, however, was not prejudicial. Quite the contrary, if you asked the student himself. Not least for the happiness that now live in their own apartment in the big city. Far from the tobacco plantations and the wicked stepparents. He had actually drawn a winning ticket.

Yin for the day in the exclusive Ray-Ban sunglasses and newly acquired beige linen trousers with matching nut-brown sweater and a pair of white Nikes. Moreover, with a stroller in front of him ...!? Zhinsun in green hat, gray hooded sweatshirt and carrying that blue fabric bag ... no bottom. Both attentively but discreetly peering around him in crowds. When suddenly ... out of nowhere ... Yang came walking straight towards them. With a freshly caught handbag hanging in the gap. A black sleek and shiny Gucci in exchange for a piece of candy quickly relegated down under the blanket in the stroller. On top of which is also the dog then homely and with a light hop jumped up. So obviously undramatic and content yawning after the completion of a mission. Once back comfortably in his favorite place on top of the baby blanket in the otherwise still empty stroller. The two then went quietly on through the arrivals hall as if nothing happened. Among the passengers from a train had just received Yin suddenly see a young girl of her own age. Of the confused gaze and unsafe behavior, she pulled quickly concluded that it was a girl from the country. An innocent angel in worn blue jeans and t-shirt. A fearful and doubtful such whose first courageous step reluctantly took her through the crowds and echoing loudspeaker sound. Meanwhile lug on a battered old suitcase ...

———

ISBN: 978-91-7463-768-7